Dio's Detective A

Sue,

Glad you liked
The Blog stories —

Here are The longer
ones

Beri

0.0 of Flagon
7/10/08

Acknowledgments

Dio and Flagon have been racing around in my head and on paper for quite a while now. They have both undergone transformations over time, and a number of people and places have been instrumental in these changes.

In particular, I would like to thank the cowboys of the Yahoo SCOX financial board, a group of programmers and other technical people who were very supportive of the early Flagon days, both with links to my work, and in one case, a place to put it. Several of the character names come from nyms on that board including Poncewaddle, who spent a lot of time in the beginning checking for updates at the Delaware courthouse. Other nyms pop up in the stories on occasion.

The second group is the people of Yahoo 360, the first blog of the Flagon universe short stories. Much of that work is now being transferred to www.flagonsworkshop.com, Flagon's newest home.

Lastly, there are the writers of www.Worth1000.com (Yes, there is a text section at Worth). This is a good place to hone one's skills, as well as get honest critiques. Everybody was helpful, but I would like to single out Jago, for his single-minded insistence that I get my quote punctuation right. I use a lot of them, and it was a help, though it took at least six months to get into the habit of doing it correctly. I don't know which of us got more frustrated during the process.

Lastly, there are the direct contributors, some of whom will show up in a number of my books.

'Celestial', whom I have known through the years, undertook the thankless task of editing behind me. (No one likes cleaning up after the dragon.)

'Wannabe' (K. Springer) from Worth1000 who illustrated the front cover. If anybody should be designing book covers, he should.

And so the journey begins...

Contents

The Tireless Caper

I was sitting in my office, cooling my heels and drinking a bourbon and water. Of course, with the drought going on, we were told to conserve water, and like the good citizen I am, I obey government regulations. Tomorrow I would add the water. The dame who does my greeting for me was cleaning out my colt 45.

"Don't blame me. Your friend Kangaroo was by and he cleaned you out of that. I am just getting rid of the cans," Flagon said.

"Did he say what he wanted?" I asked.

"Some chips to go with the beer. He made do," Flagon replied.

I checked my snack drawer. Yeah, he had made do. He better have some good information for me next time we meet. The Kangaroo was OK, just watch out for your beer and snacks. We probably would have found him watching the TV if it hadn't been repossessed last week. I came to an agreement with the store. I would continue not paying them, they would cart off the TV at their expense. There wasn't anything I wanted to watch anyway.

Flagon was one hot dame. Sultry voice and a figure that just wouldn't quit. She somehow had gotten behind me - never let a dame do that - and was reading the script over my shoulder.

"I think we need to make a few changes in that," she suggested.

"Why, sweetheart?" I asked.

"For the sake of your continued existence," she pointed out.

Well she still held all the cards, including my loaded gat, so I decided to humor her. Then the phone rang.

"Dio's detective agency. No crime too small, no fee too large. Dio speaking." It was the police commissioner. He calls me in for the hard cases. The ones his boys can't handle.

"Pastrami on Rye? Yeah, I can find that for you. Anything else? Got it. Let me check my calendar." I looked at the blank appointment book from last year. I reminded myself to get a new one. "Yeah, I had a cancellation for this afternoon. I can get on it immediately." I hung up the phone.

"So what is the caper?" Flagon asked. "Aside from bringing his nibs his lunch that is."

"Big one," I replied. "There was a massive theft of police equipment, and he wants me to check it out."

"OK, so what got lifted?"

"Tires," I said.

"Tires?" Flagon asked.

"Yeah, from a police car when the officer was making a pinch."

"Let me get this straight. Somebody stole the tires from a police car while the officer was on the street making an arrest? Did they get the battery too?"

"I don't do assault on batteries," I said flatly.

Flagon winced. "Look, we save the universe, clean out black holes, battle super beings, and the commissioner is hiring us to track down some tires? Explain to me why we are taking this case?"

Just then, the lights went out. "Oh yeah, I forgot about that," Flagon said.

"None of that woman," I said. "It is probably just a city wide black out."

Flagon looked across the street. "Lights are on over there."

"Must be our block," I lipped.

Flagon looked down. "Street lights on our side are working." I stuck my hat on my head and retrieved my gun. Hopefully, some day I would be able to afford bullets for it. We left the office.

"Lights are on in the hallway," Flagon pointed out.

"Quiet, woman, I am thinking about more important things." Like I said, Flagon was one hot dame. I stopped at the hall corner, picked up the fire extinguisher, and put out the fire in the seat of my suit. I thoughtfully had had it tailored in asbestos. Never hire a dragon as a secretary. If you do, never let her stand behind you.

We got to the corner deli. "Pastrami on Rye," I said.

"Let's see some cash first," Ira, the proprietor said.

"This one is for the commissioner. Put it on his tab."

"Dio, the commissioner is the only one in the city who is a bigger deadbeat than you are," Ira pointed out.

"Looks like you are due for another sanitation inspection," I observed.

"The graft in this city. You can't stay an honest businessman around here!" Ira said as he prepared the commissioner's lunch. Ira kidded a lot, but he would take a bullet for me. To be specific, he would take a bullet, load his gun, and take a pot shot at me. Luckily I know how to duck.

We left the store and walked into city hall through the front door and past the complaint desk.

"Do they get many complaints?" Flagon asked.

"Apparently, however, they have not listened to a single one," I observed.

We arrived at the commissioner's office. I informed the secretary I had an important meeting scheduled with the commissioner, and she let us in to his inner sanctum. I handed him his lunch.

"What do I owe you?" The commissioner asked.

"Nothing," I said. "You owe Ira a pass on his next city health inspection." Just then, a cockroach scurried out of the bag and started doing a mamba on the pickle.

The commissioner shrugged. "This is a big one Dio," he said. "You think you are up to it?"

"I am up for anything," I said. "What is the payoff?"

"You keep 10% of the tires you recover."

"The guy at the aluminum recycling center cuts us a better deal than that," Flagon pointed out.

"Yeah, but you have to go through garbage cans to get that," the commissioner replied.

Flagon took a quick look around his office. "And your point would be?" She asked.

"We will take the job," I said. "So where is the crime scene?"

"4th and main in the financial district," the commissioner said. "Officer Murphy will brief you when you get there."

We left the office. "What do you think?" I asked Flagon.

"I think the cockroach can find a better new home," Flagon said, as she pulled off the latex gloves she used when she shook the commissioner's hand.

We prepared to get in the car parked in the red zone and speed off to the crime scene.

"Car?" Flagon asked. "You mean you made that payment after all?"

"I'll get to it. The bent coat hanger routine is not working anyway. You got 35 cents for the bus?" I asked.

"Sure, if you have my paycheck," Flagon said. "How many blocks to the crime scene?" I asked.

"Fifteen," pointed out Flagon.

"Nice day for a walk," I said as we set out through the sleet, hail, and driving rain.

We walked a while past a bunch of seedy, run down buildings. "These places ought to be condemned and boarded up," I said.

"Why, were we considering squatting in one of them?" Flagon asked.

Just what I needed a smart-mouth dame. Particularly when she was right.

We walked past a group of men industriously holding the front steps down with their fannies. Flagon got her usual quota of ogling, wolf whistling, and catcalls. "Hey babe, why don't you dump that wimp and trade up to a real man?" One of them called. Flagon ignored him. Another chimed in "Hey momma, looking for a hot time?" I winced. I knew what came next. Oh well, another day, another lesson learned.

"Oh, in the worst way," Flagon purred. There were general sentiments of "All right dude!" and "Go get it man!" from the gentlemen on the stoop.

I smelled the smell and got way out of the way. I had already been burned once for the day, and I like to stick to a quota. Flagon has this thing she does. I never did understand exactly how she managed it, but the steps started heating up without any visible sign of flame. Oh, I knew it was there all right, you just could not see it. Anyway, there was the smell of rapidly heating brick, and shortly thereafter, the smell a pizza makes when you put it in the oven. The group quickly figured out the warmth in their nether regions had nothing to do with thoughts of a future encounter, and they decided, discretion being the better part of valor, to bravely bugger off in all directions.

Eventually we made our way to the outskirts of the financial district. It looked about the same as the blocks we had just passed, except the lowlife was sitting IN the buildings, rather than loitering on the front steps. One of the local kids was working his usual street corner.

"How is business today?" I asked.

"Not good mon. The whole city is full of deadbeats. I ain't made a dime all day."

"So what would it cost to rent your business for the day?" I asked.

"I'll take a quarter, cash up front," the kid said.

"So young, so trusting," I muttered. "Pay the man, Flagon." She dug a quarter out from... well where she had hidden it and gave it to him. He handed over the sign.

"Can I watch?" The kid asked.

"Sure, why not. Just stay out of the way," I replied.

"The usual scam?" Flagon said.

"Yep," I said, holding the sign upside down.

We got our first 'customer'. He craned his head sideways to read the sign. Helpfully, Flagon picked him up by his feet and held him upside down so he could read it. Regrettably, all the change fell out of his pockets. Flagon turned him upside up, set him on his feet and dusted him off. He was in a hurry to get away for some reason and left his change. Undoubtedly, he had an important meeting to attend. I cleaned up the change. The city was having another antilittering campaign, and I did not want to see him get a citation. We repeated the process 10 more times in the next hour, and the take came to $48.62. Not a bad morning's work. The kid shook his head, obviously impressed.

"Mon, you guys are pros," he said.

I gave him his sign back and tipped him a buck. Hell, I was having a good day and wanted to spread the karma.

"You want to work with me missy?" The kid asked Flagon.

"Sorry, I already have a paying gig."

Heck, I was feeling so good; I even paid her back pay.

"You forgot the quarter rent," Flagon said.

Ingrate, I handed her the extra quarter. We marched on, eventually reaching the scene of the crime. There were the cars all right, but no officer Murphy. "Figures," I said.

"Maybe he is chasing down a hardened criminal," Flagon suggested.

"Maybe, but with Murphy, he is more likely to be chasing down a hard-boiled pickled bar egg. Let's examine the cars anyway." We took a closer look.

Flagon scratched her head in disbelief. "Well there is certainly something you don't see everyday." There was a piece of paper under the windshield. "Note from the thieves?" She asked as I read it.

"In a way," I replied. "It's a towing notice for an abandoned vehicle."

Flagon peered in the car. "It looks intact aside from the tires," she said. "The radio is there, and is flashing, so the battery is still intact."

"The car hasn't been broken into that I can tell," I said. I used a tool I had to pop open the trunk.

"Are you supposed to have that?" Flagon asked.

"It was given to me in appreciation," I replied.

"I am pretty sure I don't want to hear the story behind that," Flagon surmised.

"Nah, it would make you an accessory after the fact," I said.

I popped open the trunk of the police cruiser. It contained about what I would expect to be in Murphy's trunk, shotgun, unfired; flares, a dozen stale doughnuts, and a case of brew. "Nothing missing here," I said, and shut the trunk.

"You want to pop this one open too?" Flagon asked.

"Any reason to?" I inquired.

"There is a banging noise coming from it and a muffled 'help, help' for starters," Flagon said.

"I don't like to tamper with a crime scene more than necessary," I replied.

"Did it occur to you it might be a witness, and you might want to question them?" Flagon asked as the banging grew louder.

I shrugged. Maybe she was right. You have to be on occasion anyway; law of averages. I popped the trunk. There was a guy trussed up like a turkey. Flagon removed the gag, a rubber chicken that was stuffed in his mouth. "So who were these clowns?" I asked.

"Which ones? The guy that kidnapped me, the cop, or the guys who stole the tires?" The guy in the trunk said.

"Let's start at the beginning," I suggested.

"I was born at a very early age," he said.

"I think he meant the beginning of how you got stuffed in the trunk," Flagon suggested.

"Oh, that, I was repossessed," he replied.

"I don't get it," Flagon said.

"I had an operation and could not pay for it," he explained.

Flagon looked at me puzzled.

"The doctor gets paid either way. If you don't have the money, there are plenty of other things you have," I said.

"I still don't get it."

"He was being taken to a chop shop for spare parts," I replied. "Then the car he was riding in was stripped."

"Let me get this straight: The 'repo' man came for him but was behind on his payments, so they chopped the car up for parts?"

"That is what it looks like. Notice that, unlike the police car, this one has been gutted."

"So why did they take the tires off the police car?" Flagon asked.

I shrugged. "Maybe they didn't feel like being chased. Maybe it was their sense of humor," I said.

"Sense of humor?"

I held up the rubber chicken. "Oh yeah, I forgot," Flagon said. "So are we going to turn him loose?"

"Free a 'repo' object? No thanks. We leave things the way we found them, and call the authorities." Flagon stuffed him back into the trunk and shut it.

"OK, so are we going to call the authorities now?" She asked.

"No pay phones work in this area," I said.

'Use your cell phone," she suggested.

"Reception is lousy here," I replied.

"Right, and I suppose it is any better elsewhere?" Flagon figured.

"It will be as soon as I pay the bill," I replied. "Let's find Murphy," I suggested, not wanting to dwell on the subject.

"So, any idea where?" Flagon asked.

"He has to be around here somewhere," I calculated.

"How do you know that?"

"Murphy, and walking? You have got to be kidding."

"So do you have any idea where he is?" Flagon asked.

"Where, yes, which one, no," I replied inscrutably.

Flagon shrugged. She probably did not want to know until she had to. She was right. We went to hunt down Murphy. Finding Murphy is easy, at least in theory. You walk around in ever widening circles from the place he was last seen, checking each bar, pub and doughnut shop along the way until you locate him. Unfortunately, in our city, there is one of those every 10 feet or so. The remaining storefronts are usually pawnshops or banks, which amount to the same thing around here. Anyway, we started out, stopping at each location. At the Fuzzy Lion, they had seen him all right, but it was a while ago.

"He was here, along with this other guy. They had a pint apiece and left," the proprietor said.

(Same answer at Joe's Corner Bar, Harry's Hideout ["If your wife calls, we never saw you"], and Jim's Bar and Grill.)

"Man, this guy likes to spread the love around," Flagon observed.

At the Peacock and Pumpernickel, the trail started getting warm.

"Where in the heck are you coming up with these names Dio?" Flagon asked. "Better yet, never mind."

"Yeah, Murphy was here about an hour ago. Had a 'repo' man with him too, nasty little character that one. They left to get doughnuts," Andrew, the proprietor, said.

We walked out. "Well that is Murphy Law," I said.

"Don't you mean Murphy's Law," Flagon asked.

"That, too, but that is Murphy's name, Officer Murphy Law."

"Hoo boy!" Flagon said.

We got to the doughnut shop. Murphy had been there about a half hour ago. They didn't know where he had gone after that though.

"Another dead end?" Flagon said.

"No, Sweetheart, a new beginning. He left a trail," I said, pointing at the ground. There was a trail of doughnut crumbs.

"Dio, that was a doughnut shop we just left. Don't you think there might be some crumbs in front of it?"

"In this city, there are crumbs everywhere," I grumbled. "But they usually do not stagger around like that."

Indeed the trail was no straight line. We followed it... right into the water. I was ankle deep in it.

"Shall I go back to the office and get the scuba gear boss?"

"It's in that pawn shop a ways back," I said. "I don't have enough to spring it anyway."

We checked in at the corner newsstand. Joey was fuming. "How the heck am I going to keep these newspapers dry?" He complained.

"Have you told the authorities of the problem?" Flagon asked.

"I told Murphy; fat, lot of good that does. Catastrophes seem to follow him around," Joey said.

"Do tell," Flagon said.

"Any idea where he is now?" I asked.

"Corner Bar," Joey said.

"Of course, where else?" Flagon muttered.

On the way to the bar, we came across the reason for the water problem. A couple of neighborhood youths had opened all the fire hydrants and were standing there as if daring someone to do something about it.

"Are they cooling off?" Flagon asked.

"More likely they are doing their laundry," I said. "Money gets Sooo dirty." Flagon picked a dry $100 bill from the muck.

"Better be putting that down before you get hurt sister." One of the bigger ones said. I left Flagon to play with her new playmates. Behind me I could hear the cheerful sounds of screaming, shouting, and swearing. I reached the bar. Murphy was sitting on a stool about knee deep in water.

"Top of the morning to you," he said.

"Hi, Murphy, about this water..."

"Yeah, I know, I was just going to take care of it. The 7th street gang should about be done with their business anyway."

"Actually, I believe Flagon has taken care of that already," I said, gazing at the rapidly receding water.

"Good girl, that Flagon," Murphy slurred.

13

"Well, I'll be seeing you later," a dark little weasel like man said. It could only be the 'repo' man.

"You left a package in your trunk you know," I said.

"The towing company will take care of that. It does cut into my profit though," he said.

"And what were you doing examining the cars?" Murphy asked.

"The commissioner asked me to look into it," I replied.

"I have this case well in hand; I don't need any gumshoe's help," Murphy huffed.

"Tell it to the commissioner," I replied. "I am only earning my fee." We returned to where I had last seen Flagon. The water had drained away at this point, and Flagon had done her civic responsibility picking up all the paper 'litter' with the pictures of the deceased presidents and putting them, um, where she puts such things. She left the bodies where they lay, though. I made a mental note to ask for my cut later. Murphy started writing out tickets.

"Vandalism?" Flagon asked.

"Loitering," Murphy corrected. We chatted as we walked back to his cruiser.

"So Murphy, do you have any leads for us?" I asked.

"Don't bet on the ponies," Murphy advised, who suddenly smelled 'that smell', the one of Flagon heating up. He might not think much of me, but Flagon scared the bezeezus out of him. Go figure

"So what did you want to know gumshoe?" He asked.

"What happened would be a good start," I pointed out.

"I got a hot tip that a kidnapping had taken place. I saw a car that matched the description and stopped it. It turned out to be John, and he had all the proper paperwork. I apologized for the inconvenience and gave him all his papers back."

"This 'John' has a last name?" I asked.

"Doe," Murphy replied.

"Figures," Flagon muttered.

"So how did the cars get stripped with you in them?" I asked.

"Well, the commissioner told us to stay on good terms with the local businessmen, so I offered to buy him a pint for his troubles. When we got back, the cars were as you found them."

"Then what?" I wondered.

"We decided to drown our sorrows while awaiting assistance," he said.

You went on a two day bender," Flagon pointed out.

14

"The man has a hollow leg, what can I say?" Murphy shrugged.

"So was it a random gang heist, or did they pick those vehicles specifically?" I queried.

"I think there was something in Mr. Doe's car he didn't want to talk about," Murphy said. "A man has a right to his own business."

"So why did they nick your tires?" Flagon asked.

"I don't think the gentlemen wanted to chance being followed," Murphy replied.

We reached the cars just as the tow trucks arrived. We said goodbye to Murphy, and decided on our own transportation home. Despite Flagon's large windfall on 7th street, we took the bus home, on my dime no less. Cheapskate.

"Did you want to stop by the power company?" Flagon asked.

"Why?" I replied puzzled.

"Your power is off due to nonpayment, remember? I know you always like to be in the dark, but I thought it might help to shed some light on this case," Flagon explained.

"It might, but I am temporarily short on funds, and there are other methods of taking care of the problem," I replied.

"My treat," Flagon said

"Save it for other things," I replied gruffly.

We arrived at our building. I led the way to the basement. We entered the electrical room. Flagon just shook her head at the condition of the wires, which were all over the place, some with clothes hanging from them.

"I wonder how much the bribe to the electrical inspector cost for this one," she said as I took care of business.

"That's OK, it is included in my rent," I said.

"Which you haven't paid in 3 months," Flagon pointed out.

Details, whatever, we left the room after I made the necessary wiring changes and ran straight into the landlord in the hallway.

"Just the man I wanted to see," Jake said, sharpening his canines.

"How much we owe Jake?" Flagon asked.

Jake was taken aback. "12 big ones," he said.

Flagon counted out the money and handed it to him.

"You want a receipt for that?" Jake asked.

"Slip it under the door if we are not in," Flagon said. We started upstairs.

It was humiliating as hell to owe the dame money. Flagon read my mind.

"Don't worry, just pay me back when you get the money for this case," she said.

I shrugged my shoulders. As long as I was being humiliated, I might as well try to borrow a couple of sawbucks. I got smacked across the hallway. They say it never hurts to ask. Boy, are they wrong. We got to the office. There were two goons waiting for us.

"The boss wants you should get off this case." The one who could walk without his knuckles dragging said. The other one picked me up by the neck so I could hear him better.

"Oh goodie, a lead!" Flagon said.

"Sister, I suggest you be elsewhere," the knuckle dragger said. And there I was with no way to get out of the way of the crossfire. There turned out to be no need for worry; Flagon made quick work of them.

"So, gentlemen, who sent you?" I asked.

"We tell you; we are dead," the one said.

Flagon started doing her nails. There is something about a dame with long nails, particularly two feet long razor-sharp ones.

They talked all right, but they didn't know much. Apparently, a gopher had hired them, paid them from a large manila envelope. We let them go, because, as Flagon pointed out, janitorial help is expensive, and it is tough getting blood out of the carpets anyway.

We entered the office. There next to the wall was my best friend, aside from the one in my bottom desk drawer with my pistol, my computer: Portal to knowledge, Gateway to the Universe. I received it from a grateful client for solving a case.

"You won it in an all night poker game from a guy who was bluffing with a busted flush," Flagon reminded me.

"No, I think that is where we obtained the toilet," I corrected.

"Oh, yeah, I had forgotten how it got its name. This one was the guy with the crooked straight…"

Sometimes Flagon has too good a memory.

"Shall we get started?" I said, as I sat at the keyboard. Flagon looked at the equipment dubiously.

"Dio, have you ever thought of trading this piece of junk in on a newer model?" She asked.

"And pay for it how? With my good looks?" I replied.

"OK, I get the point," Flagon replied. "How about trading it in for a good plastic surgeon."

I ignored it and booted up the computer. I usually ended booting it out the door, but hopefully my luck was better today.

16

"What brand is this anyway?" Flagon asked. "An early model," I replied. "It's a classic."

"I'm sure," Flagon replied. "Is it supposed to smoke like that?" She asked.

"Part of the boot up process," I replied. "Nothing to worry about."

"Is it supposed to glow red like that?" Flagon continued.

"The monitor sometimes does that," I commented.

"I was talking about the CPU case," Flagon pointed out.

Just then the whole thing erupted into flames and lava started pouring out the casing.

"Those old Duodenum chips did tend to run hot," I observed, as I calmly ran like a madman to the window and opened it. Flagon gathered up the whole mess and trotted over, dropping it out the window. We heard a scream from below. Flagon looked down.

"We appear to have nailed the landlord," she observed. "Well you just saved 12 big ones," I said. I always like to look on the bright side.

"Where to now?" Asked Flagon.

"We need some info," I replied. I placed my gun in the drawer. I felt naked without it ("Perish the thought," Flagon muttered) but it couldn't be helped.

"Where is this guy anyway?" Flagon asked.

"In a high security correctional institution," I replied.

I took one last look around; we headed out making a short side trip to Jake's office. He thoughtfully hadn't changed the locks, so I used a spare key I had 'borrowed' another time and let us in. He would have wanted it that way. Flagon's money was on the desk. She picked it up and stuffed it back where it belonged, after which I thoughtfully dusted the desk and the doorknob for Jake. One can never be too tidy. Besides, I still wasn't absolutely certain the falling computer had done him in. We went outside. It turned out I needn't have worried. The rescue equipment and the Flatfoots had already started arriving. I figured this was as good a time as any to start a road trip. We made our way up the street. The fifth estate's finest had started arriving in mass.

"Any idea what happened bud?" One of them asked me.

"Yeah, this flaming thing dropped out of the sky, without warning. Jake was leaving the building at exactly the wrong moment."

"Well it is the last time he will ever make that mistake," the reporter said. "So you think it was a meteor?"

"I have no idea, but that is sure what it looked like," I replied half honestly, anyway. I count those moments as testaments to my fine character.

"And your name would be?" The reporter asked.

"John Doe," I replied.

"I meet up with a lot of those," the reporter muttered and turned to locate more of the human-interest angle.

We started on our way. "Better wipe your feet," Flagon said. "I think you stepped in some human interest, and you are leaving a trail."

I looked down. "Yeah, you are right," I said, as I wiped off my shoe bottoms. No use giving your enemies a way to find you, particularly from the back.

"So tell me about this informant," Flagon said.

"Mitch the snitch," I replied. He is a useful source of information. They keep him locked up for his own safety.

Flagon looked at our surroundings. "I don't remember any prisons in this direction."

"Prisons are where you find them," I answered.

"Zen like, very Zen-like Dio. You've been studying behind my back?"

"Me, nah, just natural talent," I replied. We soon reached our destination.

"Dio that's a school!" Flagon said unnecessarily, and then noticed the chain link fence, the barbed wire, and the sign. "That IS a school, isn't it?" She asked.

"One of the worst types," I replied.

"What, correctional? Problem children? Gangs?" Flagon asked.

"All of the above," I said. "It is a junior high," Flagon shuddered. "Are we safe going in here?"

"Danger is my middle name," I replied.

"I was thinking more of your nickname 'Old Yellowbelly'," Flagon remarked.

I ignored her. We made our way to the entrance.

"No food or drink," Flagon read. "But does that last part mean weapons are or are not permitted?

"I am not sure," I admitted. "I have never tried though."

We were frisked at the front door. For some reason they spent a LOT more time frisking Flagon than they did me. I think they stopped when they noticed the second-degree burns forming on their hands. Anyway, after we passed through the metal detector and x-ray machines, we were allowed in. We were both given name tags, and told under no circumstances should we remove them. I asked where I might find Mitch

18

the Snitch. I got a funny look from the guard, who directed me to a classroom. We started down the hall.

"What are these guys afraid of, spitball fights? Paper Clip Wars?" Flagon asked.

Then we turned the corner, and ran into the gang.

"Well, what do we have here?" One of them said, practically drooling. "A couple of nerds it seems. Got some hall toll money nerds?" He continued.

One of the other gang members turned white as a sheet. "Don't screw with them Frankie, I know them."

"They don't look so tough," Frankie said, unconvinced.

"You weren't on 7th street yesterday, I was. Don't mess with them."

Frankie made up his mind, pulled a switchblade out of his pocket and opened it. "So which of you two is supposedly the tough one?" He asked. Flagon stepped forward. "I imagine they searched you pretty good," Frankie said, motioning with his knife. This isn't going to be a fair fight sister."

"You are so right," Flagon replied. "They searched me until their little hands blistered."

"What is that supposed to mean?" Frankie asked, then noticed his knife was glowing red-hot. He dropped it in a hurry. There was the smell of scorched flesh.

"Looks like you overdid it a bit Flagon," I observed.

Frankie was furious, and reached into his back pocket.

"NO, DON'T!" The gang member screamed. "We were all packing yesterday. It didn't help."

"Shut up. That dame is going to get what is coming to her," Frankie growled.

Flagon's eyes had turned red, her skin was turning greenish and scaly, and lets just say she was showing signs of badly needing a manicure. "Go ahead punk, make your move," she challenged.

Frankie's resolve wavered a bit, and then he was saved by the bell. An assistant principal came around the corner, flanked by two armed guards.

"Here, here, what is going on?" The man asked.

"These students were just helping us locate a classroom," I lied through my teeth. "I hope we didn't get them into any trouble."

"They won't be if they get to class, NOW!" The man said. The gang disbursed to go to class, or to look like it anyway. Go figure.

19

"So which classroom are you trying to reach?" The man asked.

"Ms. Hamilton's," I replied.

"Well, they were giving you the right directions anyway. It is right down this hall. Anyone in particular you are here to meet?"

"Mitch the Snitch," I said, handing over a piece of paper the commissioner would have signed himself if he had the time. Fortunately, I am good at that sort of thing. The man looked it over and shook his head.

"If Mitch does not start being more careful, we are going to fine him with a permanent swirly."

"A what?" asked Flagon.

"A swirly is when they stick your head in the toilet and flush it," I explained.

"OK, and a permanent one would be?"

"They 'accidentally' forget to remove your head when the tank starts refilling."

"Cute," Flagon said. "Mitch hasn't been harmed has he?" She asked the man.

"More of a warning than anything else," the man said. "He is fine."

We arrived at the door to the classroom.

Mitch was sitting on a chair, his head poking through the hole of another chair. They were the kind of chairs made out of molded plastic in many unsavory colors that regularly festooned junior high classrooms these days. One would assume they were the low bid on the contract, or from a contract won by a relative of the Mayor.

Mitch looked like a prizefighter on the losing end of a boxing match. A team of 'experts' was getting him ready for the next round.

"So, Mitch, bobbed when you should have weaved I see," I observed.

"Yeah gumshoe, some days go like that," Mitch replied

"Well, Mitch," our guide said, "are you going to tell me what happened this time?"

"Aw, you know I am accident prone Mr. Brown," Mitch replied. "I wasn't looking where I was going, and ran into this chair."

"Head first I see," Mr. Brown replied, not believing a word of it.

"I think I tripped over something," Mitch said.

"Like someone's foot?" Mr. Brown asked.

"Maybe, it all happened so fast I am not sure," Mitch replied.

Brown shook his head. "Mitch, Mitch, how am I supposed to help you if you don't confide in me?"

"Nothing to talk about," Mitch said.

"You keep this up, they are going to raise our liability insurance rates you know," Mr. Brown chuckled.

"Ha ha," agreed Mitch.

At that point, Mr. Brown's cell phone went off. "Brown here... uh uh, be right on it. You folks will have to excuse me, one of our more mischievous lads set fire to a trash can in the boys' room."

We watched him and his escort leave.

Mitch sighed. "What can I do for you gumshoe?" He asked.

"I need some info," I said.

"Don't you always. My retainer account is getting kind of low though, and I have all sorts of expenses," Mitch pointed out.

"We will refill it," I promised. "I imagine hall passes are getting more expensive these days."

"You don't know the half of it. But, um, Dio, you aren't exactly the most reliable source of cash in the city you know."

"Mitch, have I ever let you down?" I asked, sounding hurt.

"Oh come on, Dio, I got plenty of free time at the moment. You want me to count all the times?"

"I have it," Flagon said.

Mitch nodded. "Nice work with the 7th street gang. I heard about that. Never seen them so scared in my life. OK, you I trust. What do you need to know gumshoe?"

"Someone pinched some tires off a police car the other day," I said.

"Yeah, Murphy's. I heard about it," Mitch said.

"Any leads as to who pulled the caper?" I asked.

"Yeah, and you are not going to like it," Mitch said.

"I already don't," I said, "so what do you know?"

"There is a rogue cop on the force who hates the commissioner's guts. He is planning a lot bigger things than the Murphy caper to make the commissioner look bad," Mitch said.

"That has happened before," I pointed out, "what is so bad about this one?"

"It's the commissioner's kid who is doing it," Mitch said. "The kid joined the force because daddy wanted his kid to follow in his footsteps."

"But the commissioner does not have a son... uh oh," I said, the light dawning on me. He didn't. He had a daughter. And she wanted to be an actress. He decided she had to go into the force instead. "You are killing me you know Mitch," I pointed out.

21

"Yeah, well I don't make the news, I just report it," Mitch returned. "But I would love to see it from a safe distance, of course, when you tell daddy what his little girl is up to. Good luck, you are going to need it," Mitch said.

~~~~~~~~~~~~~~~~~~~~~~~~~~~~~~~~~~

We left the school. "Thoughts?" Flagon asked.

"You mean aside from suicidal?" I replied.

Flagon shrugged. "Not a bad use for them," she pointed out.

"Pardon?" I queried.

She just pointed at the sign. It said "'SLOW', speed bumps," and had a stylized picture of a couple of students. I had to admit she was right.

"So what is the history?" Flagon asked as I was stalling picking a destination.

"Pardon?" I asked.

"I know you have to have her in that little black book of yours Dio," Flagon accused.

"Have who?" I asked innocently.

"The commissioners daughter, who else?" Flagon said, exasperated.

"Oh, Melissa. We were just friends," I said.

"Yeah, sure. So what does she look like?" Flagon asked.

"Well, sort of straight laced if you must know," I replied.

"Hmm… she wants to be an actress, and she is having tires stolen off the police cars. A regular Audrey Hepburn I see," Flagon said.

"Well, she has her moments," I admitted.

"So what went wrong?"

"She always kept making the handcuffs too tight, I mean, we just sort of drifted apart," I said.

"I see," said Flagon. "Well I think we need to visit her."

"You mean at the police station of course," I replied. Just then we passed the police parking lot.

"Hoo boy!" Flagon said, "all of them."

"It doesn't look to me like she missed any either," I said.

"Well, you can't talk to her about it at the police station. We are going to have to meet her at home," Flagon pointed out.

"This would be a very, very bad idea," I thought. Dodging Melissa's knives and Flagon's flames would be a real stunt, and I had the idea I was going to get caught in the middle. "I think I need to call first, and darn, my cell phone is not working," I said.

"Oh, look, what a lucky break. There is the office where we can pay the bill," Flagon pointed out.

"You have done so much on this case already," I said.
"Get Into The Store," Flagon said, eyes smoldering. We went in, she paid and made sure we had a dial tone before we left.

"So call," Flagon said. I gulped and dialed Melissa's number.

"Do they still call it 'dialing'?" Flagon asked.

"To the best of my knowledge, you just don't use a dial anymore," I said. Just my luck, Melissa answered. I realized belatedly, I should have called any number but that one. Oh well, Flagon would have figured it out soon enough, might as well get it over with.

"Now be your usual suave self," Flagon advised.

"Hello, Melissa, it is Dio... yes THAT Dio. I was just wondering if you were free. Oh, you still charge... Well, maybe another time. I just wanted to talk about old tires, er times anyway... OK, see you then." I disconnected. "She will see us, er me," I said.

"Us," Flagon corrected. "I might get more out of her if you aren't there," I pointed out.

"That's what I am afraid of," Flagon said. "Besides, she might have company."

"She said she was alone," I pointed out.

"Yeah, alone with her knives, sharpening them," Flagon said. Apparently Flagon knew Melissa better than I thought.

Despite my best efforts to stall, we arrived at Melissa's apartment. I knocked, she opened the door.

Melissa was dressed, or at least half dressed, in a police uniform. It was an… interesting effect.

I felt distinct warmth from my backside. Normally this would be a good thing, but Flagon was standing behind me, so I think I knew the cause.

"So, Dio, who is the competition?" Melissa purred.

"My secretary, Flagon," I replied.

"Whatever, come in," Melissa said.

"Nothing, she means nothing," I mouthed over my shoulder to Flagon, as I started smelling THAT smell. So we went in. The door shut behind us revealing a couple of goons. Oh well, Flagon already was warmed up for the occasion.

"So gumshoe, you mentioned tires," Melissa said. "Want to explain?"

23

"A number of tires have gone missing off police cars recently," I said.

"Fine, so what is that to me?" Melissa asked.

"An informed source fingered you as the culprit," Flagon interrupted.

"Thanks, I will take care of the leak. Anything else?" Melissa asked.

"We weren't tasked with finding out who," I explained. "Frankly, I could care less. We were only asked to stop it and get the tires returned."

Melissa thought for a minute. "I was just doing it to torque daddy anyway, and I really don't want to mess with her," she said, pointing at Flagon. "But what's in it for me?"

"I can be your best friend for life, or never bother you again, your choice," I tried.

"Try again," Melissa suggested. I had to think quickly. Flagon could take care of Melissa and friends without a problem, but I would have to explain the mess to the commissioner afterwards, and that I did not need. "Tell you what, how would you like to pull off the most audacious crime ever heard of?"

"Talk to me tiger," Melissa said. I explained. Melissa giggled. I'd never heard her do that before. "Deal, Dio. I don't know how you plan to pull it off, but I am game."

~~~~~~~~~~~~~~~~~~~~~~~~~~~~~~~~~~~~

Flagon and I arrived back at the office. The phone rang. It was the commissioner. Seems the tires were all put back on the police cars, and he had my pay.

"I don't know how you did it Dio, but I will keep you in mind for the next time," he said.

"Thanks commish. What's that? Now the tires got stolen off of WHAT? Can't imagine how that could happen. Well, good day."

Flagon had replaced our TV set with one from the pawnshop and turned it on. The talking heads were having a field day, discussing the first crime on the moon. They were all in a tizzy trying to come up with new ways of saying "We have no idea what happened."

The current moon mission had a LEM (Lunar Exploration Module). That module was now sitting on cinder blocks, with the tires removed.

Flagon chuckled. "So what did you get for them?"

"The tires I had to give to Melissa, it was part of the bargain. You should see what I got for the hubcaps though..."

"I can imagine," Flagon laughed. "Take a girl to dinner?"

"Sure, did you have anyplace in mind?"

"There is a new restaurant on the corner called 'The Toasted Knight'..."

"What the heck," I figured. "I owed her one anyway."

The Case of the Vandalized Painting

I was sitting in my office, throwing cards at my hat. It had been a long time since my last job - a very long time. Flagon, my part time secretary and full time dragon was doing some kind of secretarial work. I was never certain what, but oh the way she did it. Well, work wasn't going to come to me, particularly since I hadn't paid the phone bill, so I needed to go out to find it. I found that while the phone might bring in a few leads, it also was the source of dozens of dunning messages daily, and just was not worth the hassle. I emptied the hat of cards, placed it on my head, and we headed out.

"Where to, boss?"

"To buy a paper," I replied.

"You are not going to retrieve one from the trash can like you always do? I am impressed."

"I was watching out the window. The trash cans have all been emptied for the day."

"I knew there had to be a good reason," Flagon said.

I ignored her. On the way out we met the landlord, who must be watching for us these days. Jasper was even more annoying than Jake had been in the way he insisted on getting paid. I figured I was paying him what the place was worth, and he owed me some change, though I could never convince him of that.

"Dio, you deadbeat, where is my rent?" He fumed.

"I paid you last month," I replied.

"If by 'last month' you mean three months ago, you are correct. You are not on the quarterly plan however. Now cough up some cash or I will have you evicted."

I knew he didn't mean it. Beneath that gruff exterior Jasper had a heart of gold. That and tenants who were six months behind who needed to be evicted first. I figured I had around three months to go.

"Now Jasper, I always end up paying you don't I? In fact, I am on my way out to secure my next case."

"With your bookie no doubt."

"Right, like you think HE extended me a credit line?" I responded.

That stopped him long enough for us to make our timely exit. We made our way to the corner street stand. Joey greeted me in his usual cheerful manner.

"Hi Dio! Where is the money you owe me?"

I hear that a lot these days; I have no idea why. "Next week, Joey, I promise."

"Yeah, yeah, like I don't hear that every week from you."

"Anyway, I need a paper."

"And I need a quarter. Cough up, gumshoe."

"Pay the man Flagon," I said.

"Oh no, not this time. You haven't paid me in two months either."

I got this hurt look on my face, but no one was buying it. I dug into my pocket and pulled out a quarter. "Emergency stash," I explained. Joey didn't care, he handed me the paper. I started reading it on the way back to the office.

"Lost and found classifieds as usual?" Flagon asked.

"Hey, I have found some good leads there!" I said.

Flagon borrowed the first section, and didn't want to hear about the nickel rent for it. Cheapskate. "Looks like the mayor is having a crack-down," she said.

On what?" I asked.

"On crack-downs, if I am reading this correctly."

We arrived back at the office, which was locked. With a new lock. A high security one.

"Nice of Jasper to upgrade the building security at no extra charge," Flagon said.

"It would be nicer if he provided us a key," I pointed out. "Somehow I think that if I ask him for one, I am going to be laughed at."

"So poof us 10 minutes into the past, and let's go in," Flagon pointed out.

The original lock was there, I unlocked it; we went in. Kangaroo was sitting on the sofa, swigging my beer and munching on a bag of cheese sticks. Well, at least he was the one person in the city to whom I did not owe money. Kangaroo, in this plane of existence, was just that - a kangaroo, though he was a master of cross-species disguise like most of the creatures I knew visiting this haven of a planet. His human form walked with a slight limp, probably because he couldn't use his tail as a counterweight. What Kangaroo was in no-time space, I never had quite pinned down.

"Dio! Got a job for you."

Well that was promising. With kangaroo, though, you never knew what you were getting into. "So what kind of gig is it?"

"Millionaire art collector."

"I suppose he wants someone to find a stolen painting for him, and he wants the best."

"No, he knows exactly where the painting is. It was vandalized. He wants it fixed."

I figured I knew where this was heading, and I am not sure I wanted any part of it. Changing history is not something to be taken lightly, one had to be very careful, and there still were side effects you were not expecting. "So why doesn't he just hire an art restoration expert?" I said, already knowing the answer.

"Damage can't be undone. He needs someone to go back to the source and stop it from happening."

"How far back might that be?" I asked.

"Er, about 800 years, give or take a fortnight."

"Did you tell him I charge by the century?"

"I didn't tell him much of anything other than you could do it. I also told him of the possible consequences of changing history, though he didn't seem much impressed."

"That isn't surprising. What is his name?"

"Lord Jonathan Livermore III."

"And by what name does he know you? For that matter, how did you get to know him at all?"

"Mr. Kang A. Roo."

Flagon winced. "You should have chosen 'John Doe'. It is all the rage these days."

"And you know him how?" I persisted.

"I pose as an art critic; pretty good at it, too, since I have spoken with most of the artists involved. The art shows throw some pretty spectacular spreads..."

"And you make sure there will not be leftovers, how considerate," Flagon commented.

"So what can you tell me about the artist and how the painting got damaged?"

"The artist was one Edward VonGruberman. He did exactly six pictures; they are noted for seemingly showing five dimensions on a 2-D canvas. You don't look at them, you look INTO them. Except for the damaged one. That one is covered with purple paint. Oh, Edward, of course is the nom de plume of Poncewaddle. This painting was owned by Baron Munchford back in spring of 1203. It, along with several others, was part of an art heist. At the time, they thought it was an inside job. The Baron paid the ransom, and they all came back intact - with the

28

exception of one, which had purple paint thrown on it. Nobody knows why or who, for that matter."

"I take it that the vandalism impacts the price of this one."

"Yes, the other five sell at auction in the $350 million range; this one fetches around $50,000. The real issue is that people LIKE to look at VonGruberman's paintings, and they are in short supply."

"Any chance of getting Poncewaddle to paint a replacement?" I asked.

"He is on to other things, so I doubt it."

"I didn't realize Uncle Poncewaddle had any artistic ability in him. Dragons usually don't," Flagon observed.

"Well he had 20,000 years to perfect his technique. He was trying for six dimensions, but anyone who looked at them went crazy."

"I can imagine," I said. "Old Poncewaddle does have that effect on people. How did this Lawrence fellow become owner of the painting?"

"He is very secretive about that. In fact, finding the whereabouts of any of Poncewaddle's paintings is difficult at best. Collectors tend to hide them."

"But he confided in you..."

"He sensed I might be able to help him."

"Well, I suppose we'd better go meet this Lawrence of yours." There was a banging at the door. The landlord must have heard us. "Say, you wouldn't happen to have a spare $12,000 would you?" I asked Kangaroo, but the ingrate had already disappeared.

We got past the landlord with the usual combination of grace, charm, and the promise of immediate payment. I pointed out he needed better locks on the doors, that one proved not to be much of a challenge. He wandered off in search of the locksmith that sold him the device.

Smelling impending money, Flagon offered to spring for the bus tickets. A good thing, since the ritzy part of town was nowhere within walking distance of here. It turned out it was barely within walking distance of any bus stop, but one has to make do.

We approached the small European county Lord Livermore had by way of an estate, and, after a lengthy delay at the gatehouse, were allowed entrance. Frankly, I don't think they liked our looks; we were escorted by a number of gentlemen who were impeccably dressed, but had suspicious bulges about the shoulders and waistbands. I had no interest in finding out if they were congenital defects or very large caliber guns, though I strongly suspected the latter. We were ushered into Lord Livermore's study, and told to wait "without touching anything." Well I was interested in picking up some clues as to Livermore's personality, but it seems that with the one-way mirrors, electronic bugs and tiny cameras, I had enough to go on already.

Livermore finally arrived, sat at his desk, and looked us over. Flagon he looked at appreciatively, the look he gave me was one he would give a cockroach that had scurried out from under his desk. "I assume you two know why I asked you here," he said.

"Mr. Roo told us you had a painting that needed restoring, and that normal methods would not work," I replied.

"And he told me you could travel through time," Livermore said.

I like a man who puts his cards on the table. It saves me a lot of investigative work. Particularly the free kind. "We can. Do you understand the implications of that?"

"I am hiring you to do a job, Dio. How you do that is your business. I am offering five million dollars, five thousand payable as a retainer, the rest due when you deliver the goods."

"Then you do not understand the implications," I replied. "The damage that was done to this painting 800 years ago. Either I have to prevent that damage, or have another copy of the painting done."

"Don't you think I have tried that? Nobody can duplicate this thing, regardless of price".

"Nobody ever bothered asking the original artist."

"The original artist has been dead at least 700 years now, so the point is... I get your point. Why not just grab the original and bring it here?"

"Two words: Paradoxes and Doppelgangers. Neither of which you want to mess with. What I am proposing is dangerous enough. For starters, do you know the chain of ownership of this painting and will it being undamaged change it?"

"I got it from a collection of confiscated paintings. Apparently nobody in the government managed to look at them, because a second painting by Edward was among the loot. Someone else bought that one sight unseen. The paintings and other artwork were 'appropriated' from a monastery, where they resided for at least 600 years, so, no, whether the painting is damaged or not shouldn't change anything."

"Good. Then I have good news and bad news. The good news is I can do it, and for far less than five million; the bad news is my retainer is fifty thousand, plus about one hundred thousand in expenses."

"How did you come up with those amounts?"

"Fifty thousand covers my back payments to everyone; the rest I need to outfit for the job, particularly money from 800 years ago."

"It shouldn't take a hundred thousand to live like a king in those days."

"It didn't. But I need to take it back in gold. They aren't going to think much of green pieces of paper issued by countries that don't exist yet."

"I see your point. One other question. Why don't you just go back two weeks and buy a ticket with winning lottery numbers?"

"Because I wouldn't have won it without time travel, and that is EXACTLY the type of thing you do not do lightly. I am only taking this on because having a good copy of the painting outweighs the risks."

"So why not come back for the rest of your five million when you complete the job?"

"I don't really need it, and you would never pay it to me."

"I am a man of my word, Dio."

"I am sure you are, but, in this case, you never would have given it."

"I don't follow you."

"If I am successful, you open that crate and find an undamaged Edward VonGruberman painting. There is no reason for you to look up Roo, and even less reason to try to hire me. You will not remember today because it never happened and that's what comes from changing history. Are you beginning to understand now?"

Livermore rang a bell and a scientist-looking type entered the room. Strangely enough I recognized him. He was a theoretical physicist who works with the interactions of matter on the wave level. Livermore hired some good help, it seemed.

"So, does what he is saying make any sense?" He asked the newcomer.

"Very much so, which is why I advised against this project. Since he understands all the implications, I believe he can indeed travel through time. As he himself said though, he can't guarantee the results you want, only that he can stop the vandalism that occurred at that point in time. If you really want this done, he is the one to do it, and he is correct; if he is successful, neither you nor I are going to remember this meeting, because, at that point, it never happened."

"Very well," Livermore said, taking out his checkbook. "I am making this out for $250,000, and there is no coming back to the well for more. Understood?"

I agreed, and he handed me the check.

"Any idea how long this will take?" He asked.

"That is not an easy question to answer. From your point of view, it will take about a week, assuming everything turns out as planned. But at that point, you will forget that week because it never happened that way. It will be an entirely different week where you are not waiting for an undamaged VonGruberman. From my point of view, a couple of months, depending on how close I land to the actual date the theft occurred. Nobody can pin down that date accurately."

"Then the sooner you get started..."

"True," I said, as Flagon and I got up and left.

"It will take at least a week for that check to clear." Flagon observed as we entered my bank.

She had a point; I didn't exactly have the world's largest balance or the best credit rating

"Sign it over to me," Flagon said. "I have the funds to cover at least $150,000 of it; we will deal with the last $100,000 later.

I made a mental note to give her a raise, or at least give her the back pay. Money in briefcase, we started out of the bank. Two unsavory-looking types started following; then one got a good look at Flagon and waved the other one off. Apparently she was getting a reputation, although the mayor, as usual, was taking all the credit for the lowered crime rate in our area.

The first stop on the list was Seymour, the precious metals dealer. Seymour was always happy to see me, or, more likely, Flagon, when I had cash. Today he was in luck. We entered his vault-like store and were greeted by his two 'helpers' who looked like they could bend gold coins in half with their bare hands.

"Dio," Seymour said, "what brings you here this fine morning?"

"I need gold, Seymour."

"You and half the city."

"I have the money to pay for it."

"Well that certainly is different. What did you need?

"I need 30 8-ounce gold bars. They need to look like they were manufactured 800 years ago, and need the exact same metal content - no other alloys."

"In other words, something completely untraceable. Can I see the cash?"

Flagon flopped the briefcase on the counter and opened it. Seymour put on his jeweler's magnifiers, and randomly checked some bills.

32

"Looks legit to me, but I will have to run it through the verifier. I will work up an invoice while I am at it. May I?" He asked, indicating the money.

"That is what we are here for," I pointed out.

He took the briefcase in the back and shut and locked the vault door, leaving us in the company of the two goons. Not for long though; a neighborhood gang tried to rob the place. They picked a really bad morning for it.

"Everybody, hands out of pockets, and line up facing that wall," the leader said, pointing.

I knew an execution killing about to happen when I saw one, but I also smelled dragon heating up, and I figured that wall would be as safe a place to be as any. Seymour's goons also complied. They were carrying pistols, the intruders were sporting Uzi's and they knew Seymour would have his finger on the panic button anyway. Playing the odds said this was their best chance to stay alive. They didn't know the gang had cut phone lines and electricity to the burglar alarm. Seymour watched from the back. There was not much else to do. He saw the heavy drilling tool plus the TNT, so he knew what came next; there just was nothing to do about it.

One of the robbers noticed Flagon was not complying. "You, too, honey. You picked the wrong time to be here."

"One of us did," Flagon purred coolly, and started transforming.

There is something I can't understand about that. The transformation is not all that fast. You would think that, among the eight of them, one of the robbers would have had the presence of mind to at least try to spray the room with lead in Flagon's direction. They never do. I think there is some sort of hypnotic component of watching a girl turn into a dragon before your eyes. All I can tell you is once that transformation is complete, it is too late to do anything, aside maybe to get measured for a coffin.

Then it is over in a whirlwind of rapidly moving dragon and robber parts. By the time Seymour's two goons had turned around, there appeared to be a bewildered Flagon amid a pile of spare arms and legs, the previous owner's having no further use for them.

"What HAPPENED?" One of them asked.

"I think a wasp got into the room, and they over-reacted," I lied unconvincingly. In any case, I wandered out of the store to find the circuit breakers and reset everything.

The one person who actually HAD seen Flagon transform was

33

Seymour, and he was busy making the sign of the cross and uttering some completely useless incantations. His better nature eventually took over since we had obviously just saved his butt, and he erased the tape from the security camera and went about coming up with an estimate for us, one considerably lower then he had originally been ready to offer. He gave us the estimate and told us it would take around four days to put our order together. We had about $20,000 left over, and set out to get the rest of our supplies.

After we left, he called the police and the recycling people. There were a lot of valuable internal organs there, and he didn't think the former owners would mind. The police, when they finally got there, took some notes, then left, scratching their heads. The robbers were all wanted men with prices on their heads, and they didn't want to delve too far into the cause of their demise. The recycling people got what they needed and gave Seymour a check for $25,000, then took away the remnants of Flagon's party.

Meanwhile we had a seamstress to visit for suitable period clothes. Martha ran a nice little shop specializing in costume dress. She had a great feel for the fabric and, more importantly, I didn't owe her anything. In this town, that was a rare combination for me.

"Got a job for you," I said.

"I can always use a paying job. What did you have in mind?" Martha asked.

I need a couple of period costumes from the 13th century. They have to look authentic and more importantly, have to use only those materials available at the time."

"That, of course, will cost extra," Martha pointed out.

"I am prepared to pay it, in cash, up front."

"So as whom do you want to dress?" Martha asked.

"I need a charlatan/alchemist costume," I stated.

"That is fitting," Martha snickered.

"Flagon needs to be dressed as a scullery maid," I said, ignoring her.

"Ahem," Flagon said.

"I mean cook's assistant," I amended.

"Got you," Martha said, "and when do you need this?"

"Friday works, if you can do it by then," I replied.

"For three thousand I can do that," Martha said.

I paid her, and we were on our way. We spent the afternoon paying all the people to whom I owed money. In the beginning, I had to

34

search for them. Word got out quickly, though, and they started finding me. We ended up with Jasper.

"You better not have run out, gumshoe."

"Oh ye of little faith," I said. "So what do I owe you - including three months in advance?"

"12 beans and… Did you mention three months in advance?" He said, sounding incredulous.

I imagine he didn't get many requests like that. "In advance," I confirmed.

"May I ask why?" He said, still not quite believing it.

"I am going to be out of town for three months, and I would like the office to still be mine when I get back" I said.

That he understood. And he came back with a number, which I paid him.

There wasn't much to do while we waited for our supplies to be assembled. We tried the public library for historical information on the painting, and got nothing. We eventually decided to pay a visit to Poncewaddle.

He was sitting in front of his view portal, sipping ambrosia and munching on toasted knights. They say with age comes wisdom. Poncewaddle was well over 30,000 years old, which made me wonder how old he was going to get. I asked him about the painting and he remembered it. He also remembered who defaced it, particularly since he had him chained to a wall. Poncewaddle is peculiar like that. He doesn't like something undone, which he had just done. For jollies, I tried to talk him into repainting it, though I knew what that would get me. So, anyway, I started to interrogate the poor wretch who defaced the painting.

Being chained to a wall for 800 years tends to make one talkative, though not about anything anyone is likely to want to hear. This guy had enough presence of mind left to remember the event.

They had stolen the paintings for ransom, but he also had a personal grudge against the Baron Munchford, something about a defiled female family member. In any case, he knew this painting was special to the Baron, so he ruined it. He never considered who the artist might have been. He had 800 years to reconsider that gaffe. He was a stable boy; the rest of the gang consisted of the butler (who else?), the coachman, and an unscrupulous art dealer who was perfectly prepared to sell the paintings to someone else after the ransom was paid. Nothing like being paid twice for the same heist.

The burglary went along smoothly, the troubles came about when

35

the art dealer had an argument with our wall ornament, who made the point moot with the purple can of paint.

I sensed he was at the point where if Satan were to show up and offer him a deal for his soul, he would take it just because hell could not be any worse. Poncewaddle tends to do Spring Cleaning every 1,000 years whether the castle needs it or not, so I figured his sentence could not be too much longer in any case.

If we had been creatures of time, he never would have remembered us since we were seeing him after the heist, but we were sort of in not-time here so I did a couple of card tricks to impress him. Oh, and Flagon transformed for his amusement, although Poncewaddle walked around like that all the time, sort of like wearing your underwear around the house, though I never bothered mentioning that to Poncewaddle, particularly since he had a cell with my name over it just in case I annoyed him too much.

After getting what information we could, including the exact day of the heist, we went back to the office to retrieve our supplies, changed over into costume and poofed into ancient Germany.

"So, how does my ancient German sound?" I asked when we arrived.

"You sound like Elmer Fudd on Helium," Flagon replied.

Critics.

The castle was easy enough to find. It looked like Lord Livermore's only with better central heating, and a competent staff when they were not stealing from you, which they were pretty much doing all the time. Some things never change.

Anyway, there was a line for budding alchemists, and a set of gallows for charlatans. They could have saved time by cutting out the middleman, but they did give you your 15 minutes of fame first, if you had a semi-believable story. I didn't, but I did have gold, and that probably worked even better.

The man at the desk was a surly-looking brute, who appeared to be happier watching you swing rather than listening to a story, so we were advised to make our spiel short or he would shorten it for us.

"Do you have something to show?" He grunted in our general direction.

I decided to forgo the theatrics and just get things on the table. I placed one of the gold bricks there.

A fellow standing at the side took it and ran some tests on it. "It is real" He said.

"So you had a brick of gold. What is that to me?" No-neck asked.

I figured what he meant by the past tense of that, but I ignored it. "I can produce one of these a day. Sort of like the goose and the golden egg. Of course the free gold stops if I start swinging."

No-neck grunted again. "What do you need from me?"

"Nothing. My process does not need any outside help."

"What do you get out of it?"

"My familiar and I need a place to stay. We will be willing to take up tasks in the castle to pull our own weight. I figure that after about month of getting a free gold bar a day, the Baron might start getting interested in the man that produces them, and what else he can do."

No-neck stroked his non-neck. "Just how familiar is this familiar of yours. My bet is a lot of folks would want to become 'familiar' with her."

"That would be a really bad idea. You had better make sure you have her permission first."

"Or else?"

"If you start finding guards in more pieces then expected it means someone was not following that rule."

Flagon just stood there, poker-faced, but I noticed the room was getting quite a bit hotter. No-neck looked around at his guards sweating in their armor in February in Germany and got the idea very quickly. Flagon was assigned to the kitchen, I drew the stable; it worked for me. I did not want to waste any time looking up our 'friend'. We were instructed to come back to this room at 9 a.m. every day with the next gold bar. I somehow doubted the Baron would ever see them but frankly, I could care less.

Since I was the new guy, they started me off on the ground floor. That is the stable floor. Cleaning the you-know-what, of which they seemed to have vast quantities. If I could change THAT into gold, I would be the richest man in history. Working with me was Poncewaddle's lawn ornament, whose name I learned, was Gunter. Gunter apparently took this job to watch out for his sister, Hilda, who worked as a scullery maid. A little light went off in my head on that one. I would ask Flagon about her tonight. Anyway, we got busy pitching the horse byproducts into a cart. I figured they would be used in the gardens, but frankly it wasn't my concern.

What was my concern was a group of ruffians who had just entered the room. Gunter nodded at one. I assume it was the ringleader for the upcoming heist. Somehow I would have to make sure he survived long enough to pull it off, and he wasn't helping.

"Well, well, you are the charlatan that tried to convince the boss you could create gold out of thin air," he said in a menacing voice.

"I never claimed the 'out of thin air' part," I pointed out.

"Well, let's go see, friendly like, where you do get the gold from?" He said, giving himself a manicure with his knife.

"I don't get it from anywhere, I produce it, one bar a day," I replied.

Without warning, one of his minions gave me a blow to the stomach, or would have, if I'd bothered to be there at the time. I poofed back in lying on the ground.

"You only get one chance at that." I pointed out, lying. Actually they did not get any.

"Borne, make him talk about something we want to hear," the ringleader said.

I gestured, and the air around the group was replaced with a similar volume of air 30,000 feet up. The room instantly got colder; ice formed along the outline of the exchanged volumes, and six ruffians went down clutching their throats and turning blue.

"Now, gentlemen, I don't want you ever to try that stunt again, understand? Because next time you become another load for the death cart," I said, replacing the air.

They got up, staggering, and, as soon as they could manage it, made their way out of the room, casting fearful glances over their shoulders.

"You would have been much safer killing them," Gunter pointed out honestly.

"Yes, but I need something from one of them. He tries anything else, he loses his gang."

"I know him, he will try."

I shrugged. "And I will deal with it when it happens." We got back to loading the cart.

After a while Gunter got up the courage to ask me what he really wanted to know.

"If you are such a powerful wizard, why on earth are you here?"

"For about the same reason you are," I replied. "You are here to protect your sister; I am here to protect an item. This is exactly where I need to be to do it."

"I may not be able to protect her," Gunter pointed out.

"Flagon can and yes, you are right, you would not be able to

38

protect her on your own. I will make you a deal, though, Flagon and I will watch over Hilda if you help me protect the object I need to save."

"And what is that?" Gunter asked.

"I can't say yet."

"Have I met you before?" Gunter asked.

I could see he already knew the answer and was very uncomfortable with it. "Yes, you have."

"I dreamed I was chained to a dragon's wall for something I had done. I don't know what. You entered the room with a girl who turned into a dragon."

"You remember a lot," I said. "The girl in question is Flagon."

Gunter nodded. "I will help you."

Later, I met up with Flagon and we looked over our new residence, which was a small, vermin-infested space in a loft over the stables, which did nothing to hide the odors or noises from below. I banished the vermin over to No-neck's place as a partial repayment for his friend's visit. Flagon inquired about nightclothes, which we had neglected to bring. Since both of us had 'gotten into' our work earlier today, wearing the working clothes to bed was not too inviting an idea. Flagon does sleep 'au natural' but she does it as a dragon, and a fire-breathing dragon amid all this hay was not a good idea. Particularly one that snores. I suggested she could try it without the transformation this time; she just gave me a look that said I darned well had better find suitable bedclothes. So much for that idea.

"Flagon dear, everything is closed for the night," I pointed out.

"So, you can poof to any time and date you want. Heck, go to our apartment get our bedclothes and at least seven sets of underwear. The local stuff is too scratchy."

"And if anybody notices we are wearing elasticized long johns?" I inquired.

"They will not survive to tell about it. Now go!"

I shrugged. I clearly wasn't going to win this one. I poofed to our apartment to get the requested items. I returned, Flagon grabbed her clothes, and I erected a curtain of darkness so we could get changed.

"I should have had you bring an electric blanket, too," she mentioned.

"And power it with what?" I asked.

"You would think of something," Flagon yawned, and rolled over on her side.

"Before you go into sleepy-bye land, did you happen to meet a girl

39

named Hilda today?" I asked.

"Yeah there was one. Hilda. Really pretty kid. Too pretty for her own good in these parts. I think the good Baron is taking a shine to her."

"I was afraid of that. She is the sister of the wall ornament."

"Really?" Flagon asked. "Does the wall ornament have a name?"

"Gunter. I also met the ringleader for the heist, though No-neck has a role in it too, somewhere. He wanted to know where my gold was hidden. I dissuaded him from asking; not permanently, though."

"Thas good," Flagon slurred, already half asleep. It seemed like a good idea at the time, so I joined her.

We woke up in time for our appointment with No-neck who was quite busy, scratching. I handed him the daily gold bar.

"I'd love to know where you get these," he said.

"So would a lot of people apparently," I said, pointedly. "It is not a good occupation to have."

"As I have heard," No-neck said. "Perhaps they just were not persuasive enough."

"If they had gotten any more persuasive, they would have been dead," I replied. "I don't suppose you might actually accept the fact I am indeed a wizard," No-neck snorted. "There is a first time for everything, I guess."

"And a last. Don't send anybody else after me."

"Was that supposed to be a warning?" No-neck snarled.

"The castle has plenty more vermin," I pointed out. "Where it congregates is usually none of my business." I left him there to ponder that, then went to the stables.

"You missed breakfast," Gunter pointed out.

"Some things are meant to be missed," I replied.

"Flagon was also late and caught hell for it until the head woman apparently got too close to the fire."

"I'll bet. Did anybody get any breakfast?"

"No."

"I will have a talk with Flagon about it then. No use everybody going hungry. What do they serve anyway?"

"Gruel."

"Cute. I take it gruel is liked so much, it is also served for lunch and dinner."

Gunter looked at me funny. "You say that like you were expecting something different."

"Not really. I was just hoping things were better. The way the castle is run, though, it seemed pretty obvious the menu would be quite limited. Why do you people put up with it?"

"It beats being eaten by wolves."

"I can see your point. Well, let's get working. I have a feeling they fed the left-over gruel to the horses, looking at the outcome."

We pitch forked the mess uneventfully until lunchtime, which never came.

"I think Helga wants something done about Flagon," Gunter said. "We have had our last meal until Flagon is stoned as a witch."

"Which is a really, really bad idea since you would end up wishing she was only a witch. OK, I will take care of it."

I went to the scullery where Flagon and Hilda were pretty much isolated, with a group of servants growing by the minute as Helga looked on evilly.

"What is going on here?" I asked her.

"This wench is a witch, and hexed breakfast. I refuse to cook until she is taken care of." Helga replied.

"She isn't a witch, she is my familiar, and you are beginning to annoy me," I pointed out.

"Then we will stone you both!" Helga roared, then saw the rats.

At first there were only a few, but their numbers grew rapidly. When there were 50 or so, the servants pulled back and let Helga fend for herself. It was one thing to stone someone accused of being a witch, and quite another to face a real magic user. None of them were stupid, and none really had a dog in this fight. The number of rats soon reached 100, all with beady little eyes staring straight at Helga.

"Wha-what is the meaning of this?" She demanded.

"That gruel you supply also feeds the rats, and they have gone hungry today. They really don't care why you didn't make it, only that you didn't, and they want it made. Now."

"Or what?" Helga said, not at all managing being dense, belligerent, and fearful at the same time.

I released the rats, and they swarmed her. "Or that," I said unnecessarily.

Helga screamed and swatted, making no appreciable difference in the attack. She eventually gave in and told the cook to start lunch. The rats immediately jumped off. Helga stood there bleeding though a number of bites.

"Oh, and Flagon will come in and leave as she pleases. Do you understand?" I asked.

Helga gave me a look of pure hatred but nodded assent. She wasn't entirely stupid. I dispersed the rats.

We met back at the loft, where we set up a full dinner. Tablecloth, silverware, and roast beef. Gunter smelled it and invited himself.

"Where did you get this stuff? We are never allowed to eat it."

"With all the trouble they gave us, I figured they owed us. I 'borrowed' it."

"People lose their heads for borrowing such items," Gunter replied.

"I think they have had quite enough of us already today, and would prefer to look elsewhere," Flagon said.

"Like going after Hilda?" Gunter asked.

I showed him the crystal orb, which tracked her. "She gets in trouble, we will be there."

"I have never been involved with a real wizard before," Gunter said, awed.

"Him? A real wizard? You have got to be kidding," Flagon snorted.

"Enough of that," I said, poofing the borrowed items back to the scullery. "Now, if you will excuse us, Gunter, it is time to turn in. We have a big day ahead of us tomorrow, it seems."

After he left Flagon asked me "Aren't you afraid of changing the future with him?"

"Poncewaddle already did," I pointed out. "You don't think he normally would have spent 800 years chained to a wall do you?"

"Any idea if he mucked with history any other way?"

"Aside from releasing six non-time paintings to the general public, no. Of course we have no idea why he did that. If he was painting for his own amusement, why give them to humans?"

Flagon pondered that. "You got me boss, but you are right, there is something fishy about that. Do we know when those paintings first surfaced?"

"No, but I was hoping to get some information from the Baron, unlikely as that sounds. He must know from where he got his painting."

"And is very unlikely to discuss that with you."

"Hence the gold bars and the other parlor tricks to get his attention. He has to know about us by now. Unless he is entirely dense, he would also guess it had something to do with that picture."

Flagon nodded. "So our next move?"

"Pay our daily respects to No-neck of course."

No-neck did not look happy to see us. He was scratching like

42

crazy now and, after the business with Helga yesterday, he had a pretty good idea as to the reason why.

"Any particular reason why you should not be hung immediately?" He asked.

"The gold, for starters," I pointed out.

"With you gone, we will find out where you are hiding it," No-neck said.

"Ah, but there is the rub. Ask yourself 'is he really a wizard or a charlatan? Let's call his bluff and see what happens.' Well what do you think? Do you feel lucky today, punk? I mean, I only command vermin and create gold; oh and choked people to death without touching them. What danger can I be?"

I put a blue aura around Flagon and myself as he was considering all that.

"What do you really want?" No-neck finally asked.

"To talk to the Baron of course."

"Will you get rid of this confounded vermin you summoned to my room?"

"Sure, if you promise to stop testing me," I replied.

"Or what?"

"Or I utterly destroy you."

"I think you vastly overestimate your powers," No-neck said.

Just then, the Baron's private guard entered the room. The captain of the guard clearly regarded No-neck with all the appreciation one gives a maggot. This was also clearly the only person No-neck really feared. I decided that was about to change.

"Well here are the two gold bars I give you every day," I said, handing them over.

"What do you mean, two...?" No-neck started, then realized what I had just done. The Captain of the guard was glaring at him. "That easy," No-neck muttered. "I can't believe you did it that easily."

"Two gold bars, eh Frederick?" The Captain said. He motioned to one of his men. "You take these two to see the Baron. Frederick and I are about to have a pleasant little discussion."

We were led off to see the Baron, as No-neck was led to the dungeon. I was really going to miss that man. Actually I would probably have to come to his rescue. I still didn't know what his role was in the plot to steal the paintings. We were taken to Munchford's private chambers, which, admittedly, floored me. The place totally disagreed with the picture I had built up of the man. It was sophisticated and gracious,

43

with even a hint of gluttony. Then Flagon spied the picture and waved me over. "Roo must never have gotten a good look at this; there are a good many more than five dimensions in it," she said.

I looked. The picture was amazing. The problem is I knew who Roo really was; he sent us back here for a reason; it is the reason I took the job. I did have to admit, the painting drew you in and made you breathless. If it was that important to him though, why didn't he just protect it to begin with? My reverie was cut short as Munchford entered the room. He was a suave, likable, well-dressed man with a ready and genuine smile. I wondered how he could preside over the mess downstairs with a clean conscience, though.

"I see you have found my masterpiece," Baron Munchford said.

"That we have. Did you get this from the artist or another collector?" I asked.

"What do you see in the painting?" Munchford asked, ignoring my question for a minute.

"The eternal struggle between order and chaos, several of the more important battles, both past and future, and a number of beings engaged in those battles. They are usually formed by the star groupings, but you have to be able to focus in different dimensions to see them clearly."

"And in this cluster down here?"

Flagon and I looked where he pointed. "Remind me to give the artist a swift kick in the rear next time I see him," Flagon said. "It isn't even my better side."

"You knew Edward then?" Munchford asked.

"He's still around. I have plenty of time to kick him," replied Flagon.

"Rumor had it he died in a fire in his studio," Munchford pointed out. "Apparently he didn't. Any idea what happened to him? I wanted to commission another work by him."

"He went home," I said. "Forget getting him to do another, he is on to other things."

Munchford nodded. "I figured as much. That particular piece of the painting is not about the distant past or the far future though it depicts a battle just about to be fought. I assume that is what you are here for. Who sent you anyway?"

That was an interesting question, since I was beginning to have my doubts about that one, too. Two many pieces were falling together for Poncewaddle not to have a talon in the pot, but he hardly would have defaced his own painting. The odds of Livermore getting his painting restored in the future were dropping a bit. Anyway, Munchford wanted an answer, and it had to be worded carefully. He had put far too much together on his own.

"A person who will eventually own the painting sent me to make sure it stays safe," I replied somewhat vaguely.

"I have no intention of selling it or giving it up," Munchford pointed out.

"Yes, but you have no intention of living another 800 years either, and that is when I was hired," I replied. He would have figured that out anyway.

"So you, Edward, and this young lady are creatures outside of time," Munchford surmised.

This guy was good. Even Livermore and his expert hadn't gotten that part. We aren't time travelers so much as time does not mean much to us. I had to be really careful of this guy. Thugs, ruffians and hellhounds were Flagons business. This kind of problem was mine.

"That is correct. When my client received the painting it was defaced. We traced its defacement back to here. We don't know exactly when or why it happens, but we do know the how, and we are here to protect it."

"Why not tell me the 'how' and I will take care of it?" Munchford asked.

"It is not something your guards will be able to handle. If you try to put a stop to it, it will still happen at some point, and I will have to spend more time finding out the when and why."

Munchford walked over to a globe, and spun it absent-absentmindedly. "So I suppose you want me to trust you?"

"It is in your best interest too, assuming you want that painting to stay undamaged."

"Well trust me a little then. Tell me the 'how'."

"A group of your servants are plotting to steal a number of your paintings for ransom. The rest get returned to you untouched. This one has a purple substance thrown all over it."

"You have identified the servants?"

"Most of them. Oh, and you need to have your captain free Frederick. He has a part in it, though I am not sure what yet. The others are the stable master, the head butler, and a stable hand who actually does the defacing, though I do not believe it was of his own volition."

"And how did you come about this knowledge?"

"VonGruberman had him chained to a dungeon wall for 800 years over it. He was quite talkative, though of course he does not remember it now since it has not happened yet. He did it because he thought you violated his sister."

"I never do that," Munchford pointed out.

"I know that - now. I hadn't met you when I talked to him. He was quite certain you did it, though, which means either someone took your form and did it, or placed false memories in his head. Either way, he was a tool, not a free agent in this."

"I take it you cannot guarantee the painting will not be defaced," Munchford said.

"If I could promise that, your guards could take care of it. I don't even know what it is we are facing."

"It is in the painting, you know."

"I didn't see it." I thought about that a bit. "Flagon, would you have a look?"

She viewed the star cluster in question. Her disguise immediately dropped, and her back scales were raised. "It is a dragon bane," she snarled. "I am not going to be very much help on this one, Dio, we have little resistance against those."

Munchford looked very composed for a person who suddenly found himself face-to-face with a dragon. "I should have figured that. It explains a lot," he said.

"What, about us or the dragon bane?" I asked.

"Both. It has already been here. In fact it has a job at the castle," Munchford said. "It is Frederick. Do you still think he should be released?"

"If he really is what you think he is, the point is moot. You are not holding him anyway."

Just then the messenger Munchford sent to the captain came back out of breath. "Sir, when I got there, the entire guard was chained to the dungeon wall, the captain was covered in purple paint, and Frederick was gone. They all must have gone insane; they were babbling about seeing the devil."

Munchford gave me a meaningful look. "Score one for your side. It looks like the battle is about to be joined."

"They need a diversion," I pointed out. "The painting he wants is in this room, and he can't steal it with us being here."

Just then, the tracking crystal raised an alarm.

"I hate it when you are right," said Flagon. She looked into the crystal. "Hilda is under attack." She showed the crystal to Munchford

46

where he saw himself supposedly about to ravage Hilda.

"Well that explains that," he said. "You have work to do. I am going to get out of this room since I have no hope of stopping him. Good luck with your assignment."

We rushed down the hallway to the scullery, Flagon not even bothering to change form. We reached it in time; 'Munchford' looked up from his 'work'. "Ah, the charlatan. I see you have brought your tame lizard with you."

Flagon roared and attacked. The dragon bane froze her in mid-air. "Much too easy," he said.

Then I hit him with my spell; his features melted first into Frederick, then into his true form. There was a deep intake of breath from all onlookers. I freed Flagon from his spell. He just laughed.

"Fools! While you have meddled here, my minions have already made off with the paintings!"

With that he disappeared.

Gunter cautiously crept out from where he was hiding. "Was that the devil?"

"No, something more evil than that I am afraid. Anyway, you know exactly what was attacking your sister now, and it wasn't the Baron. We left him upstairs when the crystal went off."

"So now what?" Gunter asked.

"Do you know where they are heading?" I asked.

"Yes."

"Then go there. We will back you up, but we cannot go in. You have an important decision to make. The history of the world depends on which path you choose. More than that, I cannot tell you."

Flagon followed at a safe distance while I went to check on Munchford. He was chained to the wall and covered with purple paint. I freed him and checked the substance out. It appeared only dangerous to items and creatures not locked in time. I had never seen it before, and would have to get some information on it at some point, but now was now.

"I take it the thing got here too fast," I said.

"Yes, it arrived moments after you left. It chained me to the wall, then threw the purple paint on me. Funny thing, though, it got some on itself and hissed and foamed some before disappearing"

"Good, it is throwing doppelgangers off all over the place then. This paint will just wash off, make sure you do so before you try to touch that painting."

"Are you sure I will ever see it again?"

"The chances are very good at this point. And now, I have things to attend to." I poofed to join Flagon. "Any word yet?"

"No," replied Flagon. "It is just going down now."

"The dragon bane is using doppelgangers. This is going to be easier than I thought."

Gunter looked the room over. There was Frederick, the stable master, the head butler and Helga, along with a couple of flunkies. There was also a man, who, judging by his clothes, could only be the art dealer. This man was clearly nervous. The paintings were all hung on the wall, the VonGruberman separated from the rest.

"I don't know why we uncrated them here. We should have just taken them to my client," the art dealer said.

"We have some unfinished business to attend to first," Frederick said. "Ah, Gunter, I hear the Baron gave your sister a really good time."

"That is what I heard, too," Gunter said grimly.

"So would you like to get even with him?" Frederick asked.

"In the worst way."

"Well take that bucket of purple paint and have at it with the picture of your choice. I suggest one that is really important to the Baron," Frederick said, looking pointedly at the VonGruberman.

"Noooo!" screamed the art dealer but he was restrained by the stable master and his flunkies.

Gunter picked up the bucket, marched toward the VonGruberman and threw the paint on Frederick.

Frederick's disguise melted off immediately and what was left was a purple-covered demon-like creature.

"Fool! You have signed your death warrant," the thing hissed.

Flagon and I entered the room, Flagon in dragon form, looking pleased. "I don't think you are going to have time for that, knowing what that purple stuff does " I pointed out.

The demon was already beginning to smoke, foam, and fade out. I put out a protective spell around Gunter just in case, but there was no need. With a final snarl he faded out of our plane of existence. Presumably Poncewaddle would know what to do with him. Meanwhile Flagon was gazing around the room.

"It appears we have some unfinished business," she said licking her chops and flexing her talons.

The occupants turned as white as the dragon bane was purple, but they were saved by the bell, more or less, when Munchford and his men showed up at the scene.

"Well isn't this cozy," he said. "Men, take them away and chain them to the dungeon wall. I will be by to talk with them later. No, not him," he told a guard as he reached for Gunter. Munchford gazed at the VonGruberman. "Your plan appears to have worked, wizard."

"Yes, when I discovered the dragon bane was creating doppelgangers of himself, the rest was easy. He was creating his own paradoxes; once that happens, it is easy to beat him. I assume that is why Poncewad… er, Edward VonGruberman hid Gunter away in a safe place all that time."

"Chained to a wall?"

"The dragon bane couldn't doppelgang him like that. It probably also explains why the dragon bane could not touch the painting in your castle - the place is a sanctuary."

"Speaking of which, let's get back to it. This is not exactly the friendliest of surroundings."

Munchford, Gunter, Hilda, Flagon and I sat down to a dinner we hadn't seen in a while, decked out in much better clothes then when we started.

"I owe you a favor, wizard, is there anything I can do for you?"

I thought about it. "I still have 27 gold bars. How about taking them and, in return, burying some local gold pieces for me."

Munchford chuckled. "You mean you really did fake the gold business?"

"I can't create something from nothing. I can move it through time and space, but I cannot create it."

"Sure, but why not just take the gold with you then?"

"The gold is worth more to you, and some gold coins will be worth much more to me 800 years in the future. Do you have any idea how much collectors pay for them?"

"So why don't you just take them with you?"

"For the same reason I don't take the picture. It creates paradoxes. The gold itself is generic, and is not likely to cause trouble. Period coins are something else again."

"OK, I will bury them in the dungeon, third level, behind the obelisk. And I will make sure Hilda and Gunter stay safe with me. I owe them. I wish you could stay, but I imagine you are needed elsewhere."

We were; we said 'goodbye' and poofed back to our own time, making a stop at the ruins of the Baron's castle. Through the sacking, and the pilfering which happened in the 14th century, the coins were there, hidden.

We then returned to the city. We checked Flagon's bank account. The extra $100,000 was of course gone, but that is why we picked up the coins. Everybody else we were still paid up, and I made a phone call to Lord Livermore. His staff did not know me from Adam, which was to be expected, but I told them I had a rare antique coin he might want to see. I described it; he wanted to see it; I was invited over.

We already knew the way and could actually afford a taxi. We arrived at the compound and were ushered in to Livermore's study. He looked us over. "You certainly don't look like coin dealers," he observed.

To settle matters, I put one of the coins on Livermore's desk, and saw his eyes grow wider. "This cannot be genuine," he said.

"I presume you have someone on the premises who can validate it."

He did. The guy looked awed; he weighted and measured, and pulled out a book of ancient coins.

"It is as it appears, an unheard-of, almost uncirculated 12th century German coin from one of the local Barons."

"Which one?" Livermore asked curiously.

"A certain Baron Munchford."

Livermore turned white. He knew that name all right.

"How did you get this?" He asked softly.

"I am going to tell you some unbelievable things. First, I need you to identify who I am," I said, and handed him my business card. He gave it to one of his security people, and we waited until they returned.

"Small-time detective, has solved a number of cases, but is usually just ahead of his creditors. There is a file on his secretary. Apparently, a number of rougher individuals are no longer around after meeting up with her."

Livermore handed back my card. Good thing too, I only had about six of them. "So what is this about?"

"You gave me the job of restoring a painting of yours. It was damaged while in the possession of Munchford in the 12th century. I was checking back to see if you received it in good condition. It is the VonGruberman."

"How do you know about that?" Livermore hissed.

"I already told you. You commissioned me for the job. I went back in time to save the painting from being damaged. You don't remember it because in this branch of history, it never happened. You received the painting intact, which is what I came here to confirm."

"Do you have any proof of any of this?"

I handed him the other item out of the bag with the coins. It was a signed and sealed letter of thanks from the Baron to Flagon and me for saving the painting.

Livermore, of course, had it tested immediately and, of course, it came back genuine. At this point he was simply stunned. "So why are you here?"

"To make sure you got the painting intact, which you did, and to ask you that I be allowed to look at it should I need to do so. It may contain important information when the time comes."

"At this point I am inclined to take your word for that," Livermore said. "So what did you want for the coin?"

"You may keep it and the letter with our compliments," I said.

We left a stunned Livermore and made our way back to our own office. I could see Flagon had a question gnawing at her.

"Back at Munchford's, you said once you knew the dragon bane was throwing off doppelgangers, he was easy to defeat. Would you mind explaining that?"

"Well, with doppelgangers, you can battle the copies forever with no effect - he just makes more. They have almost all the power of the original, and are difficult to distinguish from it. When you defeat them, they just disappear and you are that much weaker."

"I am familiar with that," Flagon said, "but I still don't get why it got easier."

"The copies are not identical to the original. You have to find the difference, and you have to have to defeat the original."

"Go on."

"In this case, it was easy. You've met Frederick many times before. It had to have been a copy, though, because your disguise did not drop. Any time you met up with the real one, it did. It got to the point you wouldn't even wear it when you were facing the creature."

"So the one with the painting had to be the original dragon banc. Go on."

"I simply needed a way to destroy it. It brought that itself, likely to use on you, me or any other non time-based creature that came to stop it. A copy threw a bucket on Munchford; it managed to get some on itself, and that was the end of it. That is why the original needed a human to do the throwing. I made sure Gunter saw what was attacking his sister so he would know exactly what to do with the paint when the time came."

Flagon nodded. "Nicely done, boss. How about dinner? My treat this time."

I should have remembered what dragons eat before I agreed. I suppose my cholesterol level will be back to normal sometime this century.

The Case of the Missing Cat

I was in one of those rare places where I didn't owe anybody anything - until next week, so could afford to let a job come to me rather than frantically looking for one. It was an unseasonably warm day in fall, and I was looking out the window contemplating a walk when I saw a society matron marching toward our building. Now, our building is not exactly an upscale office building in an upscale neighborhood, and I figured whoever the lady was she was not looking for a loan shark, pawnbroker, boiler room stock tips or the services of the working girls, which pretty much left us. I sat back down.

"Flagon," I announced, "I predict a rich woman looking for a lost article will shortly be knocking at our door. Please be ready to answer it."

Flagon looked up from her romance novel long enough to give me a 'yeah, right' look when there was a knock at the door. She slithered out of the chair in a way that should be made illegal, and opened the door.

"Hello, is this the Dio Detective Agency?" A well-dressed, well-fed middle-aged woman asked.

Flagon turned to the window on the door and pointedly gazed at the sign etched on it: 'Dio detective agency'. "Hey boss, I thought we were the Chinese laundry!" She said.

"Would you mind just letting the client in," I said, exasperated. Flagon did so.

"Good afternoon madam, I assume you are here about a lost pet."

"Why Mr. Dio, you are simply amazing; indeed I am."

Flagon was busy making retching noises in the background and giving me her 'you WILL pay for this' look. I ignored her. For now anyway. Doing it for too long gave you blisters.

"So tell me about this missing pet of yours Mrs..., well I guess we better start with your name."

"Florence Vanderbilt. And I assumed you would know about the animal in question, given your powers of observation."

"Of course, it is a cat, but I sense not a pedigreed one," I said.

"Correct again, Mr. Dio. My you are everything they said you were," Florence gushed.

Meanwhile, in the background, Flagon sat there open-mouthed, catching flies.

"Fluffy appeared at my door one evening. Well fed and well

groomed as most cats are, but with no ID or collar. I kept it, and put an ad out looking for the owner. It was an adorable cat, able to read my every mood and was intelligent, too. It soon learned how to work the pantry and even how to find the silverware. One day, I found it batting around the dial of the safe. Wouldn't you know it, Fluffy actually got it open by pure chance before the butler shooed him away. The poor thing must have been traumatized by that; he disappeared soon after."

"I take it nobody claimed him," I said.

"No, nobody ever called for him."

"My fee for finding lost animals is $10,000 plus expenses. I do not require a retainer. Is this acceptable?"

"Oh yes, anything to get little Fluffy back. But don't you want a description of him?"

"Male, white and gray markings, half Persian, half Siamese," I said.

"Thank you, Mr. Dio. Please let me know as soon as you have located him." Florence said as she left.

"OK," Flagon said, looking dangerous, "how did you know all that?"

I handed her the classified ad under 'lost and found' I had saved. "I always keep the ones that smell of money. Makes me look like a genius when one pops up."

"That it does," Flagon said as she read it. "With a name like Fluffy, I am glad it wasn't a dog, though."

"You and me both. We haven't spent any time as cats recently have we?"

"Never," replied Flagon, "might be interesting to try it."

"I want to find out a bit more about that cat, though. They aren't noted for opening safes, and the cat sounded way too interested in the valuables. Also I know a thing or two about Mr. Vanderbilt which Florence failed to mention."

"Such as?"

I pulled an old newspaper out of the filing cabinet and handed her a page. "Such as that."

Flagon read it. "Very interesting." Ambrose Vanderbilt was a scientist working on behavior modification of animals. He disappeared just before 'Fluffy' was found and he worked at a place called 'Animal Behavior Clinic', whatever that is.

"Do you think he modified Fluffy?"

"Yes, that is what I think. There is nothing more selfish than a cat and only a fool would add intelligence to it. The lab would probably be some place close to Vanderbilt's digs, too, which narrows it down."

It did indeed, although 'close' around the rich is a relative term. In any case, it was within walking distance, which was a good thing. There was a small, nondescript building with a sign "Animal Behavior Clinic."

Flagon looked doubtful. "Are you sure this is the place?"

"One way to find out," I said, and we entered the building. The lobby was nothing much to speak of - Government-issued furniture and institutional gray walls. I ran a scan on it, though. One-way mirrors, bugs, hidden video cams. Cute set up. I wondered what we were getting into.

The nondescript person at the desk gave us a nondescript greeting and asked us whom we were here to see. The nameplate on the desk was 'J. Doe'. I figured we had stumbled on a bit more than a neighborhood clinic. "We want to talk to somebody about a cat that got loose from here two weeks ago."

"Sir, I assure you all our test animals are properly handled. They do not 'get loose'."

"Really? I am sorry I bothered you, then. This particular cat is capable of opening a combination safe with its paws. It's Half Persian, Half Siamese. Are you sure you aren't missing it?"

A discrete red light starting blinking on Doe's desk. She picked up the phone, listened, hung up, and returned to us.

"It turns out a cat matching that description did escape from here two weeks ago." A door opened and four government goons marched out. "These gentlemen will take you to the person you need to see," she said.

I wasn't so sure this was so good an idea, but short of Flagon putting on a show, we sort of did not have a choice. In any case, the guy had some info we needed. Whether he would give it to us was something else again. I gave Flagon a significant glance; she started warming up just in case. The goons beckoned, we followed. We were taken to a well-appointed office with a placard on the desk that said 'Mr. J Doe - Chief of Security'. Not exactly the person with whom we wanted to speak, but you had to start somewhere. The goons gestured for us to have a seat; it seemed as good an idea as any. It wasn't long before a small, fit, balding man entered the room and sat behind the desk.

"So, Dio, interesting case history you and your assistant have," he said.

"We get around," I replied. "We are here to talk about a cat."

"We will get to that in a moment. I have some very strange tales about your assistant here. Something about turning into something fanged and fire-breathing."

"I imagine you hear all sorts of strange stories in your business," I pointed out.

"I do. But that is not a denial."

"Mr. Doe, our adversaries invent all sorts of strange stories about us. Probably because they are too embarrassed to admit what really happened to them. Saying a magical dragon beat their butt's sounds better than saying some dame out-fought them. There isn't any story I can give you that I can prove, so you will be in just as much of a quandary as you are now. The important thing at the moment is that cat. I am getting the picture that it is much more important and dangerous than anybody gives it credit for. Is Dr. Vanderbilt still here, and can we speak to him? He has to be mixed up with this."

"How are you making a connection to Dr. Vanderbilt?"

"The cat showed up first at his house. His wife, Florence, christened him 'Fluffy' and kept him as a house pet. The cat wasted no time getting open a wall combination safe. Florence thought the butler shooed him away before he got anything; I think he didn't. I think that cat found and took exactly what he was looking for. Then the cat split and wasn't heard from again."

Doe drummed his fingers on the desk. "Anything else?"

"Yes, I noticed the alley cats in the area seem to be organized into gangs. I have seen enough of the human version of gangs to know one when I see one, and they appear to have surrounded this building."

Doe came to a decision. "I take it you can be discrete?"

"In my line of business, you are either discrete or deceased."

"Keep that in mind," Doe said. "Dr Vanderbilt is here, but you can't talk to him. He is, you should forgive the phrase, 'catatonic'. He left the building, and we found him the next day wandering around as a bum, with no sign of understanding or recognizing any of us. His last subject was indeed 'Fluffy', or X7-P31 as we know him. He was working on improving cat intelligence."

It figures, I thought. "What about his notes?"

"They were all destroyed. We had thought he had done that himself. Now I am beginning to wonder. So how do you intend to find an alley cat with human intelligence who is organizing cat gangs?"

"Sort of my business," I pointed out. "What do you want done with him when I find him?"

"Bring him back here dead or alive; I don't care which. I will pay

56

you $500,000. That had also better buy your silence on the subject, or I will buy it another way. One last question: We thought we had pulled all information on Vanderbilt. Not even Florence knows. She has been getting steady letters from 'him'. How did you get hold of the info on the disappearance?"

"I managed to have a newspaper clipping from that day," I said, handing it over. "I must have gotten it before you started your clean-up."

I got the feeling Flagon just figured out how I kept coming up with those timely newspaper clippings, and it had been one of my better-kept secrets. Oh well. "OK, It is a deal. We find and deliver X7-P31 here, you verify it is the cat in question, we get a half a million. Nobody else hears about it," Doe nodded in agreement.

~~~~~~~~~~~~~~~~~~~~~~~~~~~~~~~

"You had me going with those newspaper clippings, you know," Flagon said. "Neat trick, wish I had thought of it."

I grinned. "It isn't going to help us at the moment, though. I think it's time to gain our cat-hood." We turned into an alley, made sure nobody was looking, and altered form.

"Dio, you are the scruffiest looking alley cat I have ever seen," Flagon said, just about as I was going to compliment her. "Just playing my part," I lied. We soon met up with sentries for the gang.

"Hey, hot momma, what are you doing with that mangy cur?" One said.

"Is there any species on the planet that does not do that?" I wondered. "I haven't met one yet," Flagon replied.

We were saved, more or less, by a newcomer coming on the scene. He was a large tabby with a nasty-looking scar around his neck. He was flanked by two other cats that were not particularly acting like cats.

"How many times do I have to tell you not to play with your food?" He asked our 'escort'. The other cats looked 'sheepish'. "So, what can you tell me about these two?"

"They aren't from around here," One said.

"I'll bet," Old Scar said. "Any idea where they are from?"

The cats all stared down at their claws.

"This is not a trick question. You are supposed to be watching that building. Nothing in, nothing out without me knowing about it, remember? So did they come out of there?"

"The only people entering or leaving recently were some guy and a dame," a cat volunteered.

"Did any CATS come out?"

"No."

"The two humans who came out, where did they go?"

"Into the alley in front of us."

"And where are they now?"

"They disappeared," the cat said, suddenly deciding it was time to look puzzled.

"And at the time they disappeared, these two cats appeared. Is that about right?"

The cat nodded, happy to get one right.

Scar turned to one of his henchmen. "Tiger take these... idiots and give them something less important to do. Then bring me the 9th street lookouts; they are good enough for this job." Tiger rounded up the gang and headed out. Scar and his other henchman were joined by the biggest, meanest group of alley cats I had ever seen. I could feel Flagon heating up beside me. Frankly, I was in the mood for some flaming felines myself, but no need to show our hand this early. There was still information I needed.

"Do you have a name, or do I need to call you 'Scar'?" I asked.

"I suggest not calling me that if you want to live," Scar warned.

"So what should I call you? It doesn't have to be your real name, just something to keep me from having to say 'hey you!' when I am trying to get your attention. My name is Dio, and this is Flagon. And yes, those are our real names."

Scar considered me. "Helix," he said.

"Helix, I am going to bet you were sent to find Fluffy by the lab after you had been modified to human intelligence, and were wearing an obedience collar. My bet is also that Fluffy found a way to remove it, and you are a high-level official in his organization."

"You have a good imagination, Dio. Can you guess any further?"

"No. We are in uncharted waters here. Originally I thought I was dealing with a cat with cat motives and human intelligence, which is enough of a problem. This is shaping up to be something more."

"So they sent you out to kill or capture Fluffy. What did they offer you for the job?" Helix asked.

"$500,000. Which, of course, is not even fit to line a litter box with, but they had to think they knew my motives."

"Which are?"

"Originally, just to check things out. The scope has expanded a

58

bit."

"So sad your time has contracted then," Helix purred evilly. The guard cats started moving forward, and we got a glimpse of something dark and sinister moving in behind them. I threw a time-freeze spell on them all, and Flagon and I made good our departure."

~~~~~~

"We quickly made our way back to the lab. The same receptionist was there. "We need to talk to Mr. Doe immediately," I said.

"Mr. Doe said he didn't want to see you until you had X7-P31."

"I don't have time to argue. We can either talk in his office or I can shout it out here, his choice." The goons came into the room and escorted us to Mr. Doe's office.

"This had better be good," he said.

"Actually, it is bad, and we don't have much time. You sent a second modified cat out there to track down Fluffy. It had on an obedience collar with a tracking device. You neglected to tell me about that."

Doe shrugged. "Now you know. So what?"

"Fluffy successfully removed it. That cat is part of his organization."

"That's the chance we took. So capture both of them. Same price though."

"Quit worrying about the price. Worry about this. I found out what Fluffy got from that safe. It was the Professor's notes. Fluffy has them all, and has been modifying cats ever since."

"That is not good," Doe admitted.

"This is worse. This building is about to come under attack. Get all non-essential personnel out now, update headquarters with the new information and get ready to defend yourselves."

"You realize you are becoming a pain..." Doe started, as klaxon horns suddenly went off.

"Times up," I said, and Flagon and I made our exit.

"There are cats all over the street," Flagon said. "No exit that way."

"Let's try the roof," I said. We nearly made it there when a skylight exploded and two dozen cats and a couple of the murky items dropped to the floor. We got out of there fast and made our way to a side office with a window. "Only way out," I said. Flagon kicked it open.

"Too far to jump," she pointed out.

"That leaves one exit path," I said, and Flagon and I both transformed. I got on her back, and we flew out of there. We were seen, but there was enough other weird stuff going on that nobody with a camera got it pointed in our direction in time. I cloaked us in invisibility, and we watched the rest of the show.

Whoever was making the jokes about cat herding can stop now. The cat attack was well organized. The same was not true of the human defense. There were sounds of screaming and some of the employees jumped out windows to get away from the cats. Then all of the cats streamed out, and the building exploded. I have no idea if anybody made it out.

Flagon and I landed, donned our working clothes and walked back to the office. There were a couple of government thugs waiting there for us. Bad news travels fast, it seems. They 'invited' us to take a ride, and we ended up sitting in the Police Commissioner's office. The Commissioner looked plenty scared; there was another man with him who looked to be the late-lamented Mr. Doe's boss. We were motioned to some seats; the goons stood right behind us.

"What happened?" Doe, Senior, a man of few words it seems, asked.

"Do you want me to start with our involvement, or the attack on the building?" I asked.

Doe, Sr. sat back. "Might as well give me the whole story to start with. It could save time that way."

I told him about Florence Vanderbilt and her missing cat, about how I tracked Mr. Vanderbilt to the clinic. I described our visit to the clinic and our being hired to find Fluffy. Then I told him about the second cat the clinic released, and my suspicions. Doe, Sr. sat through the whole thing without saying a word until I was done.

"Do you think you caused the attack?" He asked.

"Hard to say, sir. Those cats were already in formation to attack when we came across them. That we had been sent by the clinic may well have triggered the timing of the actual attack."

"How did you infiltrate the cats?"

"We took on cat-form," I said. I didn't see any reason to hide that at this point; it would come out anyway, and I had a feeling there was no time to spare.

"You took on another form when you left the building, didn't you?"

60

"We are shape-shifters, sir. We can take on whatever species form we wish."

"Can you impersonate somebody?"

It was my turn to consider. "Not in a way that cannot be detected. I can look like somebody but it would be obvious it is not that person."

Doe, Sr. nodded at a goon, who opened a door, and a very shopworn Mr. Doe hobbled through.

"Does that match up with what you have?" Doe, Sr. asked.

"Aside from the fact I don't trust him any further than I can throw him, yes. There are some things he is not telling us that relate to this matter."

Doe, Sr. turned to me. "Well?"

This was going to be tricky. There were some things it just would not do to tell. On the other hand, there were things that would be obvious when they sat back and talked about it. I chose my words carefully. "Sir, I run a detective agency. That means I have to track down clues and weave together the story they are telling me. I am extremely good at my job. I don't get that many jobs, I don't need them. But if somebody needs me, he finds me. This was obviously more than a 'lost cat' case from day one. Cats do not open safes. Everything else fell together."

"And you're reading now?"

"Those cats are probably the most dangerous things to hit this planet in a while. You could end up losing at least the city to them. The only person who might fully understand their abilities is in a coma, and the cats have all his notes. My reading now is that we are in deep trouble."

Doe, Sr. nodded again. "Stay where we can find you."

We left. I was wondering how it would be possible not to stay where he could find us. We made our way back to the office. Jasper was there, but so flustered by events he forgot to ask us about the rent. At that point, I knew it was serious. I plopped into my chair, and Flagon sat in hers.

"We go to find a lost cat and end up saving the city. Par for the course, isn't it?" Flagon pointed out.

"Except we haven't saved the city yet, and I am short on ideas," I replied.

"Are there any leads left to follow up?" Flagon asked.

"Yes, but I am not sure on how to go about it. That cat opening up the safe bothers me."

"It is a modified cat. Go figure."

"Yes, but you still have to make assumptions about it. For one, it should not have any abilities it did not get from either the cat or human side."

"Go on."

"Fluffy supposedly is a lab animal that never leaves the government building. It gets loose, makes a beeline for the Vanderbilt estate, which location he has no way of knowing, finds the exact safe storing the notes and opens it without a problem. I have a problem with that. It doesn't add up."

"OK, so how do we check up on it?"

"The most direct method would be to examine Ambrose Vanderbilt. Somehow, I think Doe, Sr. is not ready for that. Next-best method is to find what the good doctor was up to before that fateful day."

"I know you by now, Dio. Spill it."

"I can't impersonate someone without being detected if they are interacting. A comatose subject is a lot easier to work with. We only have Mr. Doe's word that they have Ambrose's body, and he doesn't have the imagination to believe he might have been had. I don't think that is Ambrose they have there. I think Ambrose is working with the cats for some reason. I would like to determine what that reason might be."

"Next stop?" asked Flagon.

"Cockroaches Rule."

"You mean that wacko organization devoted to finding the next dominant species for the planet? Does Ambrose have a connection to it?"

"That is what I want to find out."

~~~~~~

We arrived at 'Cockroaches Rule', a stately building on 21st Street. It had the appearance of being a gentleman's club, which it probably was. I rang the doorbell, and a doorman who looked to be Methuselah's great-uncle answered it. I asked to see the club president, and he told us to wait in the hallway. Portraits of all the founders were in the hallway, and Flagon gave me a nudge and pointed at one. Either this was a huge coincidence or Ambrose Vanderbilt was a founding member of the club. A nervous little ma in a sweater and bow tie came out to greet us.

"Hello, I am Percival Wainwright, III. Are you with the press by any chance?"

"No, sir, I am Dio, and this is my secretary, Flagon. We are here looking into the disappearance of Ambrose Vanderbilt."

"Then I am afraid I have nothing to discuss with you," Percival said.

"Percival, Ambrose was on a secret project, modifying cat behavior. Earlier today a large group of cats, attacked, overran, and blew up the Animal Behavioral Clinic where Ambrose was conducting his experiments. Some high-level Federal Security officers are very, very interested in this case because of it, and I am working with them. So, no, you don't have to discuss anything with me. The group of guys that arrives next, for them you better have a good story ready."

Percival started mopping his head with his hanky. "Well, Ambrose was sort-of a part-time member. Never really part of the organization, though."

I pointed at Ambrose's portrait hanging on the founders' wall. "I suggest you get rid of that, then. It gives a wrong impression."

Percival started mopping his head even more. "Sir, you must understand. We are a peaceful, law-abiding organization. We merely watch the decline of man and speculate over his successor; we don't do anything to bring about that change."

"That is what I am trying to find out. And yes, from what is public record about you, that is quite true. I still have a missing scientist, a destroyed government building, and an army of apparently mentally augmented cats to deal with. Now what can you tell me about Ambrose?"

"Ambrose was a founder, it is true. He had a falling out with the organization, about six months ago, over the very thing you are asking about. He felt it was well past the time for some other species to take over."

"Is that when he started working on cats?"

"Yes. He got as far as he could with the equipment he had, and he needed access to some items not available to the general public."

"It seems to me he was rich enough to get whatever he wanted."

"That was deceiving. All the property, and most of the money, belongs to his wife. While she may look like an airhead, she is not. She is a noted scientist in her own right. The marriage has been a rocky one, even at the end."

"She appeared to be more worried about that cat than about her husband," Flagon said.

"You folks have a reputation, too," Percival pointed out. "I don't think Florence picked your office at random. I think she was really scared by the whole affair, and she figured you folks stood the best chance of sorting things out in a hurry. How would you have reacted if she had told you her real concerns?"

"Point taken," I said. "I will talk to Doe about it. I can't guarantee he will not send some goons anyway. My bet is that, sooner or later, you will probably be thankful they are around. Ambrose seems to be playing for keeps, and he is not allowing anybody to get in his way."

"Florence mentioned something about getting regular letters from him."

"The previous director of the lab's doings. He thought he had a comatose Ambrose under observation. My bet is that he was wrong. Fluffy knew way too much for that." "Do you think Fluffy is Ambrose?" Percival asked.

"I have not made my mind up about that. Was Ambrose dabbling in mind transference, or just mind augmentation?"

"I don't know," admitted Percival.

"Neither do I. I am hoping Doe, Sr. does."

"Awful lot of 'Does' running around," Percival noted.

"Yeah. Too many. You'd think one of them might be named Smith or Jones, wouldn't you?"

We then took our leave.

"Where to now, boss?" Flagon asked.

"Back to the office, and put a call into Doe, Sr."

"Why not just call him from here?"

"I need to think about the new info we have, and I do that best at the office."

~~~~~~~~~~~~~~~~~~~~~~~~~~~~~~~~~~~~~~

We got back to the office and immediately the phone rang. Flagon picked up. It was Doe, Sr., of course.

"Put Dio on the phone," he commanded.

"Yes, sir," said Flagon, and she happily handed the phone over to me. I glared at her. She just smiled.

"I was expecting a report from you," he said.

"I just got back to the office. Calling you was first thing on the list. Er, did you have a name you wanted us to call you?"

"Mr. Smith will do. So, why didn't you use the cell phone?"

"Because I can't secure it, and Doe said this whole thing should be confidential."

"That didn't stop you from blabbing to Percival," he pointed out.

"I didn't tell him anything he didn't already know, and I needed him blabbing to get more information. So, if you got the whole conversation, which I figured you did, what is the fuss about?"

"The cats are on the move again."

"I figured they would be, and after the Armory now, I would imagine."

"And how would you imagine that?"

"It is pretty clear you are fighting a war, Mr. Smith. The sooner you realize that the better. They need weapons."

"They can't use them."

"Land mines, grenades, poison gases, those they can use. That armory has any of them?"

There was a pause on the other end of the line. "I understand you do not think the body we have belongs to Ambrose Vanderbilt."

"There is a strong indication of that. I need to examine the body to be sure. And if it isn't, I need to know exactly what equipment he was using for his experiments."

"Unfortunately, as you well know, the lab was flattened."

"I know that. Was Doe sending out regular reports? Did he send out an incident report for the cat getting loose? Did he report on the doctor being missing?"

"Doe's incompetence has been dealt with."

"That sounds like a big 'no' to me. Do we have anything to go on at all?"

"We have a professor, who reviewed his work two months ago. He strongly suggested Doe pull the plug on it."

"Which Doe, of course, didn't bother doing. So where is the body now?"

"We assume Ambrose perished when the building exploded."

"Assume? You mean you didn't do any DNA testing? Look, ask yourself this one: Why did the cats choose that time to attack? What where they after?"

"The notes?" Smith asked.

"They had destroyed them already."

"Stopping any further work on the subject?"

"They had no idea Doe was that incompetent. That work should have been going on in at least three different places."

"Then what? I am out of guesses."

"The body of Ambrose Vanderbilt. That is the only thing that had to exist in only that place. I was getting too close, and they needed to dispose of that evidence before I had a chance to examine it. Since I was

65

already in the building, it forced their hand."

"I think you have a puffed-up view of your own importance."

"I think I am not chained to a wall in your basement which means you are not sure how important I am, either."

It was Smith's turn to sit back and think.

"What difference does it make if Ambrose is behind this? We pretty much knew that anyway."

"If Ambrose is personally directing this mess, it simplifies things: Find him and stop him, and the felines go back to being felines. If he isn't, you have a huge problem. You will probably never be sure you got rid of all the stray cats short of nuking the city without warning."

~~~~~~

"Let's get Dr. Oppenheimer in here. He is the one who raised the warning."

Dr. Oppenheimer had the appearance of an old European scientist. Distinguished, knowledgeable, and only partially understandable.

"I don't know why you people didn't listen to me when there was time to stop this."

"We are working on that, Doctor. What we need is to go over some specific items."

"It is all in the report."

"The report was destroyed when the building went down."

"Then what did you want to know?"

Smith nodded at me. "You are up, gumshoe."

"Doctor, was Vanderbilt modifying cat intelligence, learning to mind control cats, or something else?"

"Mostly the first two. He had to alter their consciousness to do his bidding and he had to exert some kind of control over that new-found consciousness."

"You mentioned 'mostly the first two'. I take it there was a third component."

"Yes, he had to alter his own consciousness to think like a cat. A scientist using himself as a test subject is always fraught with danger. The fact he was contemplating it set up the red flags for me."

I shot Smith a meaningful glance. "Doctor, one last question: was Vanderbilt breaking new ground with this, or was he using well-known theories and equipment?"

"Scientists have been working on controlling the behavior of

66

higher-order animals since Pavlov and his dog. Things, of course, are much more refined now. The altering of cat intelligence is somewhat new, but it was tried successfully on other mammals. The third part is entirely unethical, no matter how you do it, and there is no written work on the subject.

"Thank you, Doctor, I believe I have what I need now."

Dr Oppenheimer was ushered out. Smith looked at me. "So what do we know now?"

"We know we are looking for Vanderbilt, and this silliness stops when we find him. The problem is finding someone who thinks like a cat." Flagon nodded. "Smith, I hate to give your ulcers a twinge at a time like this, but we are going to have to go missing for a day to get that answer for you."

"You realize I can track your every move?" Smith replied.

"Not this one you can't, and I don't have time to explain why. I just assure you I will return tonight."

~~~~~~~~~~~~~~~~~~~~~~~~~~~~~~

We left for the office. "You know he is only putting up with you because he needs you. We could very well get chained up to that wall when this is over."

"I think we will have to put off dealing with that until later. If I have to shut down the office, I have to. I don't think it will come to that, though."

"So where are we going to find someone who thinks like a cat?"

"I am not sure, but Kangaroo is a good place to start."

He was. The problem was, I never found him; he always found me. I suppose I could hang a right at Mars and ask for directions, but I didn't have time for it, and besides, I am male. We have this thing about asking for directions. As it turned out, it didn't make a difference. Kangaroo was already at the office when we got there, helping himself to beer and chips as usual.

The guy must have better tracking devices on us than Smith does, I thought.

"So, I am given to understand you need something that can think like a cat," Kangaroo said.

"That we do; do you know of anything like that?"

A half-cougar, half-man came out of the kitchen with another one of my beers. "Meet Milos," said Kangaroo. "He dates back to Greek times. As you are probably aware, the gods of the time were none too picky about what their progeny looked like. I figured he would be right up your alley."

"Good afternoon, Milos, has Kangaroo described the problem to you?"

"Yes, you are looking for a guy who thinks like a cat, and you need to find him pronto," Milos, said.

"Pronto?" asked Flagon.

"Hey, I keep up with the times, dragon," replied Milos. "Did you happen to notice if all the cats you were facing where any particular gender. Female, for example."

"No, there was a good mix of males in there. Why?" Flagon asked.

"If they had been all female, you would have been dealing with a lion. His majesty sits on a throne, and his wives do all the work."

"No, these are all house cats," I replied.

"You are getting your butts kicked by a bunch of Felix Domesticus? You are a sorry bunch!"

"Yeah, all house cats. Except they hunt in packs have knowledge of human devises and carry explosives," Flagon pointed out.

"And you couldn't stop them, dragon?"

"Not without taking dragon form, and that sort of blows our cover."

"Well, with that kind of cat, you are probably better off with a Sphinx cat to start with."

"I'll go get one," said Kangaroo. "Did you want me to take you back home while I am on my way?"

"Nah," said Milos, "plenty of beer and chips here. I can wait."

Just what I need, a drunken half... whatever, I thought, as we awaited Kangaroo's return. Fortunately, Kangaroo wasn't long... and he brought with him one of the weirdest cats I have ever laid eyes on.

"Greetings again folks, this is Ra."

"Of Sun God fame?" Flagon asked.

"Technically," explained Ra. "My master was a pharaoh. In death, he claimed to be the embodiment of the Sun God, typical in those days. Since I guarded his tomb, I got the moniker as is customary."

"Was he the Sun God?" asked Flagon

"He was greedy, less than an even-handed judge, and a blight on his empire," said Ra. "So he could have been the sun god. He also could have been the re-incarnation of a cold cod. Whatever."

"Well, we have a cat to worry about, not a pharaoh. Can you tell us anything about what a half-man, half-cat would be thinking?"

"If he is thinking along Egyptian lines, he will have found himself a nice hidey-hole. Preferably one that is part of a labyrinth. He will store in it what is important to him. He will use the other cats as his army, procuring what he wants for stockpiling."

"Any idea what he wants?" I asked.

"I know what I want, and it's in that drawer. I can smell it," Ra said. He proceeded to the bottom drawer of my desk and unlocked it, using his claw as a lock pick. "Hey, wizard, you got a saucer around here? I don't do well with glasses."

I found a reasonably clean coffee saucer, placed it on the floor and poured some hooch into it.

"The city is in danger, and here we are pouring 10-year-old Scotch into a saucer for a 2,000 year old Egyptian cat. This place is insane," Flagon observed unnecessarily.

"So what do you think Ambrose might be after?"

"That is your half cat?" Ra asked.

"Yes."

"Has he made any demands yet?"

"No, but he is threatening the armory. That is a place we store weapons," I said.

"My best guess would be that, if you have a museum with an Egyptian exhibit, he would be stationed in the storerooms underneath. He can't be at the armory, if he were he would already have the weapons. The only other choice would be a cloister, and this city does not appear to have any of those."

"Hmmm… I don't recall Ambrose having any Egyptian in his pedigree. Any chance we have an undead running around?" I mused.

"There is an exhibit of a tomb excavation at the museum, and I believe it contained a mummy, one of the ancient pharaohs," Flagon said.

"Any idea which one?" Ra said, suddenly interested.

"Not that I know of. It was not one of the famous ones," Flagon replied.

"If you do not mind, then I would like to stick around," Ra requested.

"Sure," I said, "just take it easy on the sauce. I don't need to squire around a drunk cat."

It was time to update Smith, and I picked up the phone. I dialed, and he answered personally. The lack of a middleman was probably not a good sign."

"You have a lead for me, I hope," Smith said. "This is about to blow up in our faces."

"I do for a change," I replied. "Check out the passages under the natural history museum, but do it quietly. A full frontal assault is exactly what we don't need right now."

"Why would Ambrose be there?"

"He is looking for a dark, out-of-the-way place. According to my informants, that appears to be it."

"Can I talk to them?" asked Smith.

"Sure, you want the Kangaroo, the half-man, half-cougar, or the 2,000 year old talking sphinx cat?"

"For my own sanity's sake, I am going to pretend you are kidding. I will have the museum checked out."

"I want to re-iterate: no frontal assault. I think it would be a trap, and I think it would trigger counter attacks all over the city. If you decide to do it anyway, make sure the guard at that armory is re-enforced first. You might also want to secure the power plant, TV stations, any potential target. Right now you have an uneasy truce going. Be sure you are ready before you break it. I am only being strident about it because I don't need you coming back at me and saying it was my idea. It isn't."

"Fair enough. How do you think the cats are using this 'truce'?"

"Preparing defenses and building up additional forces would be my guess. As I have said, you are fighting a war, and you can't afford to think about it in lesser terms."

"All right. If you come across any more info, let me know. Anything else?"

"Yes, have an ancient Egyptian historian on hand. We may well end up needing one. In particular, it would be helpful to know when that mummy arrived at the museum, and who exactly it is. That information I can use as soon as you get it."

I hung up. "I think we need to work on a command center ourselves. I don't think we can fool ourselves into thinking Ambrose does not know where this office is."

Flagon checked out the window. There were a number of beady eyes staring at her from an alleyway. "I would have to say you are right on that one, Dio."

"Can cats fly?" Kangaroo asked

"No. Ra, can that mummy teleport anything?" I asked.

"Usually not, but I need to know who it is to be sure."

"I will set up the command center, then," said Kangaroo, and poofed out.

"What now?" Flagon asked.

"We sit here and wait, I guess," I said.

"I don't like doing nothing and waiting," growled the cougar-man. "I need to get out and rend something."

"So rend a can of beer and another bag of chips," Flagon suggested.

"Cool."

I dialed the phone. Flagon looked at me quizzically. "Maybe Florence has some answers. I said. After talking to half her staff, I was finally put through to Florence.

"Do you have any information about my Fluffy?" She asked.

"Florence, we are about to have some really serious stuff going down. I know you better than that now; you didn't come see me over a lost cat."

"Well, in a way I did. What is Ambrose up to?"

"Apparently he is leader of a cat army. Tell me, did he show a sudden interest in Ancient Egypt a while back?"

"Yes. He had been non-committal to being bored by the subject until a friend took him to the new display at the museum. He came back entirely enthusiastic, but somewhat changed otherwise."

"Did he happen to know who the mummy on display was?"

"Tutus-grandmas, as I recall."

I looked over at the Sphinx who was nodding his head vigorously.

"Thanks, Florence, you have been a help. I think I know what is causing the problem now. I will be back in contact."

"The cats are moving out," Flagon said, gazing at the alley.

The phone rang. It was Kangaroo. "I suggest you get up here immediately." I poofed everybody to his location. He had a couple of wall-screen TVs going, plus some radio feeds. The TVs immediately grabbed everybody's attention.

"This just in," the announcer said. "The armory is under attack by, of all things, cats. Apparently, so is the Natural History Museum. The National Guard was called out." (Turns to look off camera) "OK, whose idea of a joke is this?"

Then the film feeds started coming in, showing soldiers under attack by cats, and not having an easy time of it. "We now have a report from Sarah Evans, down in the street near the Natural History Museum. What is going on there, Sarah?"

71

"Well, Steve, this whole thing started when a squad of elite army soldiers made a frontal attack on the basement of the museum. Apparently they had word somebody was holed up there; we are not sure. The soldiers were overcome by cats, and reinforcements have been pouring in all day. Nothing is making any headway against the cats, however."

"Our reporter on the spot at the armory is Bill Standish. Bill?"

"Steve, the armory has been lost. The cats came in through the vent-work, overpowered the guards in the grenade and poison gas storage facilities, and since that point it has been a massacre. Apparently the cats are wearing some kind of gas masks, and they are dropping grenades and poison canisters down the vent grills onto the soldiers. We are getting more troops in now to try to stop the spread of the weapons; they are setting up a defensive perimeter behind me."

"We have an important bulletin. The cats are apparently attacking this TV station. The guards downstairs are all down, and they are coming up GAH! GET OFF ME!"

The screen went black. "Nice following of directions, Smith," Flagon said to no one in particular.

Then the screen came alive again. Ambrose Vanderbilt was on it. "This is Ambrose Vanderbilt. The cats picked me to be their spokesperson since they lack the vocal apparatus needed for human speech. If you do not meet all their demands within one hour, they will continue bringing this city down around you. First, all attacks against cats must stop immediately. Second, all troops massed around the museum must disburse. Lastly, the detective, Dio should be brought to the museum and handed over to the cats. You have one hour. I think you understand what not complying means at this point." The screen went blank again.

"Hey boss, free advertising!" Flagon said cheerfully. Everybody else stopped what they were doing and looked at her. "Well it is. Er, Dio, shouldn't you update Smith.?

"Somehow I think he already knows."

"No, I mean about the mummy."

"Yeah, that will really go over well at this point. Smith, it isn't a mad scientist running the cats. It is an undead pharaoh. Flagon whose side are you on anyway?"

"Well, you are going to need to call him either way."

"True," I sighed, and I picked up the phone.

Smith, predictably, was not in the best of moods. "Dio, where are you?" He snarled.

"I am in a command center disguised as a cloud, and floating over the city."

"Remind me to stop asking questions like that," Smith said. "Well, it is a good thing you were not in your office. The cats sacked it."

"They seem to be sacking everything. I believe I gave you some advice on that."

"Yeah, well one of my superiors decided there was less risk attacking than waiting, and didn't want my view. Happily he is now having to explain it all in the Oval Office."

"It got national attention then?"

"Dio, they attacked National Guard units, then the Regular Army reinforcements. They took over a major TV station. Of course it made national news. There is probably a real question whether or not they need to nuke the place. By the way - what did you do to get on Ambrose's naughty list, anyway?"

"You said you were not going to ask that kind of question again, remember?"

"Well, you need to get down here either way. I have some people who want to talk to you, and we have that cat demand to consider."

"Nice to know you folks consider me suitable for cat-chow. All right, I will be down. My original agreement in this case was with Doe. Any idea what I am working for now? Aside from my continued existence, that is."

"I will ask about it."

"So where is 'here' these days? I assume you are not set up at the commissioner's office anymore."

"There is a loose cordon around the armory, Col Bigalow commanding. Report to him. He may need to blindfold you bringing you here."

"Lack of trust?"

"Not on my part. You have saved or tried to save our bacon too many times now. We have new people on this, though, and they would feel a lot more comfortable if you didn't know where we are."

"You do realize, you bring me there, blindfolded or not, I will know where I am."

"Yes, and I have no intention of explaining 'why' to them."

"Any objections to my bringing Flagon?"

"No, leave the menagerie at home, though. I have no intention of explaining them either."

Flagon and I arrived at the armory and were immediately surrounded by trigger-happy soldiers. We asked for Colonel Bigalow, and were taken to him. He looked us over critically. "We have been watching for anything that drives, walks, burrows, swims or flies, and you didn't do any of those to get here. Which begs the question of how you did get here."

"Colonel, with all due respect, we were told to report to you for transport. How we got here is our business; time is short, and we are wanted elsewhere. There are only 45 minutes left before the deadline."

Well, he bundled us up, blindfolded us, and handcuffed us for good measure. We were led to some kind of vehicle, plopped in unceremoniously, and taken for a drive, at least part of which was underground. There, they unloaded us like a couple of sacks of potatoes, and dumped us into two chairs in a conference room. The guards then left; nobody else was present. Flagon and I took the opportunity to shed the handcuffs, white suits and blindfolds, and sat back down after placing them in a neat pile on the table. Two men I didn't recognize came into the room flanked by Mr. Smith and a number of guards. "I thought I left orders for these two to remain bound!" one thundered.

"They were," one of the guards, replied.

"So, a couple of escape artists are we? Shall we really test your abilities?"

"Sure, as long as you can get us out in the 35 minutes you have left. Or maybe we could better spend the time discussing the problems at hand," I retorted.

"And how do I know you are not in league with the cats?" The man asked.

"Oh for pity's sake, talk to Colonel Bigalow. He has no idea how I got there. If I were in league with the cats, don't you think I could get to the museum under my own power?"

"You could just be trying to sabotage our efforts to deal with the cats."

"Except all the damage was done when you didn't follow my advice, not when you did. There were a number of places I warned your people, starting with Doe, of what was going on. I had a great problem getting people to listen to me."

"Probably because your story was so far out," the man said.

"I can't help that. It was either that or not explaining at all. Sadly it always kept me one step behind events. Like now."

"OK, so what is going on at the museum?"

"Ambrose used to be a simple nut case. Those were the 'Cockroaches Rule' days. By the way, they have nothing to do with this mess so don't waste time bothering them. Things changed when he visited the new exhibit at the museum. His mind was taken over."

"By cats?"

"No, the cats are doing the creature's bidding just like Ambrose."

"What creature?"

"Here goes," muttered Smith.

"An undead pharaoh by the name of Tutus-grandmas. Ambrose visited at the wrong time, the mummy took control. Find and destroy the mummy, and everything goes back to normal."

The man's face started turning red. "Do you expect me to believe this whole mess is being caused by the spirit of an ancient pharaoh?"

"Sir, I have worked with so many government agents on this one that I really don't care what you believe anymore. That is what is causing the problem. Deal with it now, or take your time and consequences for not believing it. Your choice. You send me into that museum, I am going to have to level it. Whether that gets the mummy or not, I don't know at this point. I will let you know when I do."

"What do you need to level the place?" Smith asked.

"I have the tools necessary as it stands."

"Why won't it kill the mummy when you do that. Strike that, I just answered my own question."

I turned to the leader of the group. "Your decision. How do you want to handle it?"

"I could just truss you up again, and take you far away from here for questioning."

"No, you can't," I replied. "I will not let you do that. I will answer any questions you ask, but you are not going to imprison me."

"Pretty strong words for a down-on-his-luck gumshoe," the man said.

Flagon heated up and transformed just a tad.

"I told you what I was willing to do. Now do you have a room for us?"

We were led down to the residential wing; meanwhile the meeting went on.

"We can't trust him. I say we put him where he never sees the sun again and throw away the key."

"Ted, you are acting like every other idiot who has been assigned

75

to this case," Smith pointed out. "Every one of them has completely missed the implications this guy is catching; he is probably the only reason we have a clue of what is going on. You keep this up I am going to get NSA involved immediately. We are out of time if you have not gathered. Now forget about Dio. Do we go after that mummy, or Andrew?"

"I don't believe the mummy exists," Ted said.

"Well if you hadn't cut off my covert team, they would have that answer for you by now. I had sent them in to gather information about the place. John overrode that and ordered the full-scale attack. With your support. So was that a right or wrong decision?"

"John paid for it."

"Indeed he did. Which means you are now on the hot seat. Obviously, the mummy considers Dio to be his biggest threat. That is why he is demanding him on a platter."

"We could still nuke the place."

"Oh, come on Ted, and explain that to the public how? 'Some cats got loose from a government installation so we nuked the place'? It gets to that, we have already lost. It means we have no hope of containing the cat army."

"So what is your suggestion?"

"We send in Dio and his friend through the front door, as requested. We send the covert operations team back in through the back door. We do not tell Dio about them. Worst comes to worst, we should have a lot of information we need."

The meeting broke up. Smith got his way, but Ted was not smiling.

~~~~~~~~~~~~~~~~~~~~~~~~~~~~~~~~~~~~~~~

Meanwhile, I just came out of a trance.

"Did Molly have any words of wisdom?" Flagon asked.

"Yes, to destroy that mummy will require fire."

"That seems easy enough."

"It would be, but we need a fire made from a holy consecrated object. A wooden cross will do."

"Give Smith a nudge?"

I glanced at my watch. "Yes, but we will be cutting it close."

"I thought you didn't need anything," Smith pointed out.

"I don't to level the place. I do to destroy the mummy."

"So what do you need?."

76

"A wooden cross that has been blessed. You need the fire from a holy relic to destroy the mummy."

"So how were you planning to ignite it?"

"I have a large economy-sized lighter," I said pointing at Flagon.

"Something else I don't want to ask about?" queried Smith.

"Yes."

"OK, let me see what I can do."

~~~~~~~~~~~~~~~~~~~~~~~~~~~~~~~~~~~~

We all met at the car about 15 minutes later, Flagon and I with our usual escort. Smith had the cross with him. Ted looked at it. "What is that for?"

"Dio said he needs it to destroy the mummy."

"Do you still believe in that stupid mummy story?"

"I believe the cross cannot cause a problem, and there was no reason not to obtain it for him."

"Look, this guy for all his talking, has shown us not one shred of mystical powers."

I took the cross and made it disappear. "No use letting the mummy know I have it in advance," I said.

Ted had sort of turned red. I do that a lot to government agents it seems.

"I'll take them on in," Smith volunteered.

"Sure, just be around to take the blame when this is over," said Ted.

We piled into the car, and it sped off.

"How much time do we have?" I asked. "We are already over the hour limit."

"They have been told you were in hiding, that we just found you, and you are on your way. Ted wanted you blindfolded and handcuffed again. I won that argument."

"Under the 'give him enough rope' theory?"

"At this point, yes. Ted is well aware some heads are going to roll no matter how this goes down; he is setting up other people's heads for the chore."

We arrived at the museum. "Do you mind if I join you?" Smith asked.

"This is going to be exceedingly dangerous," I said

"Yeah, but I wouldn't miss it for the world."

We arrived at our destination and got out of the car, which promptly drove off. There were cats everywhere watching our every move. Ambrose's voice came from a loud speaker. "If any of you are carrying weapons, put them down now."

I dropped my pistol, Flagon a derringer, and Smith assorted pieces of hardware. The cats stepped aside to let us pass. "I can't believe he would be that stupid," Flagon whispered.

"He is probably just having fun with us," I whispered back as we entered the building.

We entered through the main lobby. Smith looked up at the vents in the ceiling with a worried look. "I don't like those," he said.

"We will take care of them. Did you happen to find out where they got all the cat-sized gas masks from?"

"I was hoping you had that answer."

We progressed into the first exhibit hall and were immediately attacked from all sides. Flagon changed form and started flaming, I took the vents and a series of explosions, from grenades going off, emanated from them. In a short time the room was filled with charred cat remains and kibbled cats raining down through the ductwork.

"For a general of cats, Ambrose sure does not look like he minds wasting them," Smith observed.

"And how many soldiers did you lose today?" I asked.

"Point taken. Where to next?"

Just then, a museum screen came to life ahead of us. "Very good Dio, you have passed the first test. Can you handle the next two?" Ambrose intoned; then disappeared.

"I think he has been watching too many Grade B spy movies," Flagon said.

"Who, Ambrose or the mummy?" asked Smith.

"I doubt it was the mummy," I remarked dryly. "By the way, what is your name? Unless you enjoy being called 'Smith' anyway".

"That is my real name," replied Smith. "Andrew Smith. That idiot Doe was the only one using a cover name. Thought it gave him an advantage. I still kick myself for not seeing his incompetence any earlier."

"It's not entirely your fault. Your organization appears to have more than its share of incompetents. Doe just didn't stand out as worse than the others until he was put to the test."

"Did you get a reading on the location of the transmission?" Flagon asked.

"Two rooms straight ahead."

The doors to the first room were shut - the first such doors we had come across. I felt them. "Uh-oh," I said. "Andrew, come feel this door, and tell me what you think."

Andrew came forward and observed the door. "My booby trap detection skills could use some work, but I don't see anything obvious."

"No, I meant put your palms on it and feel it."

Andrew did so and his face turned ashen. "What is that?" He whispered.

"Zombies. They feel of dust and decay and hate of the living."

"Is it the mummy?"

"No, they are not powerful enough to be that. Probably re-animated cats and soldiers."

"So how do you fight them?"

"Crushing them works. Actually anything that reduces them to small pieces, a club even."

"So are we going to take them out?"

"No, I think wading into them would be a spectacularly bad idea. We need a way around."

"There are no side doors," remarked Flagon.

"Nor steps to the basement, though I am loath to go down there before we have to anyway. That leaves one direction that I can think of." I pulled a rope and grappling hook out of my hyper pack.

"Neat device. You wouldn't happen to have any hardware in there?"

"I think it would be a really bad idea for you to be carrying a gun," I said.

"Because?"

"The mummy can control minds. I don't need you behind me pulling your gun if you are taken possession."

Andrew gulped. I took a couple of passes at tossing the hook at the vent, not even coming close. Andrew tried also, and was a better shot than me, but he couldn't get it to stick.

"Oh for pity's sake just give it to me," Flagon said, exasperated. Andrew handed it over and Flagon transformed into dragon, took the hook up and snagged a metal post inside the vent.

"Gah!" remarked Andrew as Flagon landed.

"You guys want to ride me up, or climb the rope?"

I hopped aboard. "Andrew?" I offered my hand, he took it, and I helped him clamber aboard. Flagon flew to the vaulted ceiling and let us both off at the vent. She then took hold of the rope, changed back to human form and climbed in herself, pulling the rope up after her.

"Of course, they now know you are a dragon," Andrew pointed out.

"The mummy knew it the whole time, and Ambrose is not really conscious," I said.

We journeyed down the vent, coming to a duct over the next room. There was the sound of moaning and growling. I looked down, then motioned for Andrew to join me. Below were a multitude of undead, both cat and human, walking around with no purpose as zombies are famous for. Andrew gulped. "Well, I did ask to see all this."

"That you did. If I had just told you, would you believe it?"

"Not really," he admitted. "Do you do this kind of stuff all the time?"

"Pretty much," I admitted. "Every once in a while we get an ordinary case. It breaks the monotony."

Andrew looked at me like I had sprouted two heads. "So why are you always pan-handling with powers like this at your disposal?"

"It is part of our cover," I admitted. "I have to play the part of a down-on-my-luck, hard-boiled gum shoe. This city in this time period is going through a lot of really weird events. I don't want to be the first thing they go after every time a monster hits town."

Andrew shrugged. "Your secret is safe with me. Ted I am not so sure about."

"Those things have a habit of taking care of themselves," I observed. We passed the zombie room and exited into the next room, which contained the transmission equipment. One of the monitors came to life. Ambrose, of course.

"Impressive, Dio. You got through the second test. The third one will be quite a bit harder. And, of course, Tut-grandmas is waiting for you. Be sure you bring your pet lizard along, not that she will do you any good." The picture faded out.

"Any idea where we are going?

"We are staying right here. Apparently this one is home delivery," I said, pointing at a door in front of us that suddenly had turned glowing red. Flagon had just returned to dragon form when the door melted, and a fiery horror came through. She joined battle with it. I didn't like this. The room behind us was the zombie room, and while we could take to the vents, this kind of creature could usually fly. Flagon was holding her own, but not winning.

"A little help here, boss!"

I transformed into my wizard's robes and joined the attack with a containment spell. Whatever this thing was, it was strong, and we still were not winning. If it became a matter of endurance, I was pretty sure who had the edge. Undead creatures do not get tired. Andrew looked around. "Wizard, would your dragon be hurt by water."

"No, Flagon can get wet without a problem."

Andrew walked over to the fire alarm box and set it off. An alarm immediately sounded and shortly thereafter, a heavy stream of water hit the room. The fire beast started sputtering. Flagon blocked the door behind it while I blocked in front. The water sprinkler continued spouting and soon there was nothing left of the fire beast except for an undead corpse. Flagon sat on it with a satisfying 'squish'.

"Quick thinking there, Andrew, very well done," I said. "I believe the mummy is next. We will need to get out of this water first though."

We slogged into the next room. Tutus-grandmas were there, along with Ambrose, face set in a death mask, and a legion of undead.

"Dio, Tutus-grandmas wishes to congratulate you; you have made the grade. He will either possess you, or kill you if possession is not possible. Your dragon will be used to replace a Sphinx Cat that has gone missing. Andrew, you get to join us, too."

Andrew's features fell into a mask of possession. I was glad I hadn't handed him a gun. Flagon started fighting off the undead, leaving me to face the mummy.

"Your move, wizard," it mumbled.

I got the cross out of the pack.

"Interesting relic, but it has no effect on me," said the mummy as he started forward. In the meantime, a large number of hands reached out of the floor and secured my ankles.

"Oh, Flagon!" I said. She turned my way and set the cross on fire. The mummy saw the danger but it was a bit late for that, and he was slow moving. I felt a last-ditch attempt to control my mind as Andrew and Ambrose tried to tackle me. They didn't make it before I threw the burning cross, point first, through the chest of the mummy. It staggered around, on fire, as its legions of undead transformed back into the merely dead. Flagon took on human form. Ambrose held his head in his hands and whimpered, while Andrew just shook his head to clear it. That guy impressed me more and more.

"So how do we arrange transport home?" I asked.

"If there are no traps left, we just walk out and get my GPS phone. I can call for a ride from there," Andrew said.

"Sounds like a plan," I replied.

"One thing first. AMBROSE!" Ambrose looked up, bewildered. "Release the cats now!"

Andrew's face contorted in concentration. "It is done, master."

"Master?" Flagon asked, eyebrow raised.

"I learned a few things from that mummy which will probably prove useful," Andrew said.

We made our way out, all four of us. Andrew picked up his stuff and called for a car. It arrived, and so did the Calvary.

"Should we clean the place up, sir?" A captain asked.

"A forensic team may want a look at it fi..." Andrew started.

"Ahem," I said.

"Yes, captain. Detail what you need to clean it up now." We got into the car. "You are right, Dio, there is no way to explain what happened in there. Best to clean it up."

We got back to the command bunker. It had been breached. The signs of battle were everywhere. An underling approached us.

"Glad you are back, sir. We were attacked in your absence. Ted... didn't make it."

"Does the communication center still work."

"No sir, pretty much everything is out."

"The cats are all docile now. We took out the root of the problem. This is Ambrose. For safekeeping, stick him in a where place he can't get out. Oh, and put him under lots of sedation. I don't want him regaining consciousness, under any circumstances, until I get back. Also, start cleanup efforts and check to see what the mayor needs in the way of help. I will give you a blanket authorization. In the meantime, I am going to find a secure line so I can contact the president."

We got out of sight, then poofed to my command post. Regrettably it had also been overridden. Along with Kangaroo, the man-cougar, and Ra, there were now half a dozen elves, some fairies singing off color songs about trolls, and a group of dwarfs

Andrew just shook his head. "Dio, how do you manage to stay sane? You are sane, right?"

"So they tell me. Kangaroo, party is over, would you kindly give everybody a ride back home?"

Amid much grumbling, Kangaroo did as requested. Good thing too; I was out of beer. After everybody had left, and Flagon had made the room presentable, we switched on the communications equipment.

"Would you like to be alone for this?" I asked.

"Are you kidding? You two stay right where you are."

Andrew was soon patched through to the war room. The president looked up. "What is the situation?"

"The situation has been defused, sir. We are in clean-up mode, and determining what the damages are. My assistant director is preparing a report for you."

"Where is Ted Armstrong?"

"Dead, sir. He died when the cats attacked the command bunker."

"How did you resolve the situation?"

"The cats were under mind control. As soon as it was released, they all went back to normal."

"And the scientist that put them under control?"

"He is under heavy sedation. It is an issue we will have to deal with at some point."

"The two people with you are who?"

"Dio and Flagon, detectives. They were invaluable to solving this case."

The president nodded. "We got Doe to speak. Some very interesting stuff there. It is a good thing Ted is dead; he would be under treason charges otherwise. Apparently Ted and Doe were instrumental in getting this ball rolling. There was a foreign power very interested in the research, and they both profited handsomely."

"That brings some things I was wondering about into focus. Thank you, sir."

"Thank you. And thanks to you two. You probably saved the city. Mr. Smith will work out a suitable payment for you for your services."

We got Andrew back to his headquarters, then poofed back to our office. "It feels good to be back," Flagon said.

"Yes, but that foreign power bit is bothering me. Did they know about the mummy?"

"Not for us to care about, I shouldn't think," Flagon pointed out. The phone rang and Flagon answered it. "That was the bank."

"What, am I overdrawn already?"

"No, the government just electronically remitted $500,000 to your account."

"Well, that was the deal," I yawned… "I am ready to call this one a day."

"Capital idea wizard, capital idea."

The Midas Touch Caper

Flagon was studiously reading the latest copy of 'True Detective' and was laughing her butt off. She in theory, gave me a subscription to the magazine for Christmas though I had yet to wrestle a copy away from her to find out what was so funny. I was going though one of my lean times again. The cockroaches had long scurried elsewhere in search of crumbs, the landlord gazed at me with daggers in his eyes, and the panhandler on the corner gave me money.

There was a timid knock at the door; Flagon didn't even look up. She got that way when I was behind on her pay. The tapping on the door sounded again.

"Ahem, paying customer?" I reminded her.

"So, go answer it," she said.

"I believe that is your job," I pointed out.

She waltzed up out of her chair, having one final chuckle at my expense, and opened the door.

There, stood a little girl of about seven years old, hugging a teddy bear. That wouldn't have seemed so strange, but it was obviously a solid gold teddy bear. This could be an interesting day.

I invited her in, and she had a seat. I usually hand out candy, but the jar was mysteriously empty, and I figured a certain dragon had something to do with it.

"So, what can we do for you today?" I asked her in my serious, adult-to-child voice.

"Mister, my uncle has disappeared, and I am worried about him," she said.

"How long has he been missing?" I asked.

"About a week," she replied.

"Do your parents know about this?"

"Oh, yes, I told them."

"What did they say about it?"

"Daddy seemed a little worried, but mommy said he is an adult and can come and go as he pleases, but he never goes anywhere without telling me! I tried to tell mommy that, but she would not listen!"

"What does you uncle do for a living?"

"He is an inventor."

"And does he do well at it?"

84

"Oh yes, he owns the house we live in. Daddy is the grounds keeper and mommy is the maid."

"What was his last invention? I noticed your bear; did he make that for you?"

"Yes, he made it change color."

Flagon and I looked at each other. We each had a feeling where this was leading.

"So he was originally made of some brown material?" I asked.

"Yes. He asked me to give it to him; he put it in a funny machine, and it came out like this. I am not sure I like it, though. It isn't warm and fuzzy any more."

"And you told him that, and he left shortly afterwards?"

"Yes. Do you think I made him do that?" She asked, chin starting to tremble.

"No, honey, I think he just needed time to think about his last invention. What is your uncle's name?"

"Arthur Pessinus," the girl said.

"Did anyone come with you when you traveled here?"

"No, if mommy or daddy had known, they wouldn't have let me come."

"OK, there are some things I need to look up, so I know where I might find your uncle. There isn't much for you to do here, so amuse yourself for a little while. Flagon and I will walk you back home. It is not terribly safe for you to do that on your own. OK?"

"OK," she said, and looked around for something to do. In the meantime, I cranked up my computer to find out what I could about Arthur Pessinus.

It turned out Arthur was pretty well known. He was a scientist and inventor, and from the work he was engaged in, he would have no problem discovering the Midas Formula. Everybody who had come across it thus far went through the same bout of soul-searching, and fortunately, to date none had been found lacking. The formula itself dated back to ancient Greek times and was named after old King Midas, who found out the hard way why the world was not ready for it.

It still isn't. There is nothing wrong with the formula itself, its just its consequences are always bad, and if a person with a conscience came across it, they had to deal with it.

Anyway, Arthur had himself a string of very successful inventions and patents, and a mansion on the side of town we only got to go into, as paid help. His brother did not seem to have inherited the same genius or

85

anything else, including motivation. He wasn't a bad person, he was just never destined to make waves in the ocean of life. His wife on the other hand, was a real firecracker. She married him for his cushy job he had with his brother, and had been making designs on the family fortune and real estate ever since. There were a lot of things her husband didn't know about her, and it was probably better that way. In any case, she would be none too unhappy seeing Arthur gone, though there was nothing in her background that would indicate she would actively bring that about.

"OK, Alice, I am ready to go," I said.

She got up from where she was having an imaginary tea party with her solid-gold teddy bear. "Mister, how did you know my name?"

"I was looking up information on your uncle to see if I could get any ideas on where to find him and your name, your mommy's and your daddy's came up in that search. I should have told you; is that a problem?"

She thought. "No, anything that helps you find my uncle is OK."

We left the office and ran into Jasper, of course.

"You got my money gumshoe?" Jasper demanded.

"Working on a case now Jasper. You are first in line to be paid."

Well he was satisfied with that, for now, and we walked down the stairs and left the building.

"Mister, if you need money, you can have my teddy bear."

"No, sweetheart, that is yours. We will work out payment arrangements with your parents."

She looked dubious on that one; frankly, so was I but we were taking the job either way. "Flagon, do you suppose we might take a taxi for this one?"

Flagon considered it and agreed. Good thing, since she was the one with the loot.

The taxi dropped us off at the Pessinus residence. Alice went in ahead to announce us, and a butler came to usher us in.

Mrs. Pessinus was sitting on a couch looking for the world like the Mistress of the estate rather than the maid; I imagine she was loving it. Mr. Pessinus stood up and nervously greeted us. "Detective, I am sorry you came all the way out here, but we really do not need your services."

"From what I can see, you do," I replied. Your brother has been missing for a week."

"Arthur is a big boy now. He can come and go as he pleases," his wife said, downing a bon-bon.

"Did he let anybody know where he was going?" I asked.

"I don't see any reason we need to discuss this with you at all. We did not hire you; the butler will show you out."

"Ma'am, may I bring something to your attention first?" I asked.

"Go ahead," she said wearily.

"Your brother-in-law is missing. He gave no written instructions on how to maintain his house; who has signing authority, or when he might be back. Not being concerned about that for a week, if the missing person was not showing signs of being distraught, is no big thing. That time will stretch on, and sooner or later people are going to notice. It could be a servant, or a colleague of Arthur's, or any number of other people. One of them is going to ask the police if there has been any progress on the missing persons case. That is when the police are going to notice it never got reported."

"Now, if Arthur just wandered off and is fine, you do not have much to worry about. The police find him; he tells them he is fine, report is closed, but if he can't be found, or, worse yet, his body is found in some alleyway or unmarked grave, they are going to look for likely suspects. The first place they look, barring a direct lead, is anybody who would have profited from his disappearance. I guess you can imagine who would be on the top of that list."

"Are you accusing me of something, gumshoe?" Mrs. Pessinus asked, face livid.

"No, I am just going over the facts with you. After one week with no communication, you really need to be taking steps to find him. That would either be a private detective or a missing persons report. For your own good, you need to start a paper trail and that private detective does not have to be me; just make sure you hire somebody competent."

"Which you think you are?" Mrs. Pessinus replied, haughtily.

"Yes, I already have a good lead as to where he might be found, and his reason for disappearing. I also think he is in a place where he could easily get in trouble, and you could find his body in a dumpster. Is that what you really want?"

Frankly, Mrs. Pessinus was more uncertain than I would have liked, but Mr. Pessinus showed some backbone for a change.

"We want to find my brother. What do you charge?"

"I don't want money to be a holdup on this. Give me a $10 retainer, and if I find your brother, I will discuss my fee with him."

"Will you now give us a note saying you took the case?" Mrs. Pessinus said.

"Since that is a main point of hiring me, of course." I had the note

87

ready and signed, and handed it to Mr. Pessinus who read it over. He gave it to his wife.

"You were pretty sure of yourself, weren't you?" She asked.

"It saved time all around and cost me a piece of paper. Anything else?"

"No, just be sure to keep us updated - in writing," Mrs. Pessinus said. Apparently she had heard what I said about a paper trail.

"OK, then we will be on our way."

"One second," Mr. Pessinus asked. "You said you knew the motive; what was it?"

"Your brother came up with something that has huge moral implications. He needs time to sort things out," I said. "He needed to do that away from here, which reminds me, do you have a current picture of him? The one I have is six months old."

The one Mr. Pessinus came up with was considerably more recent, and I took it.

"I don't suppose you want another taxi ride?" Flagon said. Like she would give me one.

"No, where we are going, we do not want to show up in a taxi or a bus for that matter. On foot is best."

"So, are we overdressed for this?" Flagon asked.

"You have a point there." We ducked into an alley and changed wardrobes. The effect was not particularly gratifying, but we would fit in better this way. We did get some nasty glances hoofing it out of the Pessinus neighborhood, and we picked up a prowl car during our trip. It stopped, and the police got out. "You folks have ID?" One asked, and then got close enough to get a good look at us. "Dio, I should have figured." "Anything we should know about?"

"Not as of yet," I answered. "Simple missing persons case, no signs of foul play".

"So what is the getup for?"

"Where we need to look for him, our regular clothes would be out of place."

"Well, let us give you a ride, then."

"I'm not sure we should be showing up in a police car."

"If you are going where I think you are going, it happens all the time. We offer it as a free, one-way service to all panhandlers. The neighborhood insists on it. We will just forgo the usual stop at the station for questioning."

"As long as you put it that way..." I said, actually kind of relieved not to have to walk the whole way.

They let us off in front of the soup kitchen with a stern admonition not to be caught in that neighborhood again, else face fines and some jail time. We told them we had learned our lesson, and the police drove on.

"Lousy flatfoots," a man in ragged clothing said. "They pick you up just for walking down a street."

I shrugged. "Them that has the gold rules," I said.

We made our way into the soup kitchen line. The place was neat, and the food hot, but the clientèle tended to be a bit 'wiffy'. Frankly, I could only give the place 3 stars due to lack of ambiance.

Flagon and I picked out a table and had a seat. Everybody there was too hungry to make conversation during dinner, and the management tended to try and move people out to make room for future guests, even more of who were now lining up at the door. We must have gotten there for the 'early bird' special.

We finished up our five-course dinner, and I looked up the Maitre d' to compliment him on the fine repast. "Him" turned out to be a her, a severe looking woman in a Salvation Army uniform.

"Would you like some help with dinner, ma'am?" I asked.

"Sorry, we can't pay for help."

"You've already fed us. I was thinking more of making myself useful in return."

She looked over Flagon and me carefully. "You two aren't regulars here, are you?"

"No ma'am. The nice policeman gave us a ride in. We are from out of town."

"OK, we can always use dishwashers. Kitchen is in the back."

We tied on some aprons and got to work. The dishes were stacked up, and they just kept coming. The place soon ran out of hot water, but Flagon took care of that little problem. Somehow, we kept ahead of the crowd, with Flagon using a somewhat - augmented drying process. Finally, it was over, and the woman running the place came over.

"Great job!" She said. "If I had two more like you, we could double our dinners. Oh well, do you folks have a place to stay yet?"

"No ma'am, we are still looking for that."

"Well, I know of two; they don't allow mixed company, though. She will have to go to one and you to the other."

"That is fine for tonight ma'am, and I do have a question. We are here searching for a relative. By any chance, have you seen him? I showed her the picture.

"We don't track people down without their permission. It is sort of an unwritten rule, but I will ask around and see if he wants to be found."

"That is fine, thanks," I said.

Flagon and I went our separate ways that night. I must say my lodging was not up to my usual high standards - and those start plenty low. It was sort of a 'barracks' setting except the cots were smaller and closer together. Oh well, anything for a case. I couldn't honestly give it more than two stars, though, and that is before I saw the rest facilities. Frankly, the bus stations were a step up.

The night dragged on pleasantly with all the evening noises of snoring, coughing and cursing finally dwindling - well all except the snoring anyway, but morning came soon enough, and with it came a strengthened resolve to get this case over with as quickly as possible.

I met Flagon for breakfast, and we helped with the clean up afterward. I suddenly remembered why I hated cleaning up eggs. Eventually we got finished, apparently in record time again, and the woman running the place, who's name turned out to be Sarah, introduced us to a nervous little man.

"May I see the picture of the person you are looking for?" He asked.

I showed him Arthur. He nodded and handed it back indicating I should put it away.

"What do you want him for?" He asked.

"Two reasons: His niece, who actually hired us, is worried about him, and I think I can help with his problem."

"Which is?"

"It has to do with her teddy bear."

I could see he was thinking about it, but needed help making up his mind. "Do you have a small personal item on you?" I asked.

He pulled out a pocket watch.

"I can use that, but it will not function as a watch anymore. Do you have something that is not mechanical in nature?"

"No need. I know what you intend to do; it is enough proof for me. Let's go before I am spotted here."

I was sort of wondering how he could not be spotted here, but I let it go. We got outside and started traveling down the alley when a couple of thugs stepped out in front of us.

"Run, folks, you are not a part of this yet. It's me they're after."

Flagon looked behind us where four more thugs stepped out of their hiding place. "Sorry, I don't think they intend to let us go." She

90

started heating up.

"So, Lawrence, we meet again finally. Are you ready to take us to the king?" He said, grinning evilly while one of his gang opened up the top of a dumpster. "Or, is there going to be an extra load of garbage going out tomorrow?"

"Lawrence on the count of 'duck', I want you to duck. Understand?" I said in a whisper.

Lawrence nodded.

"I haven't run across you gentlemen before. Let me identify myself." I pulled out a 'genuine' imitation police department badge.

"So, what, you and the dame planning to arrest us all?" The leader sneered.

"No, just trying to get you to disburse or else."

"Or else what?"

I looked purposely at the dumpster. "Or else the same offer you gave to Lawrence applies."

The gang started pulling its hardware - small arms, and a number of knives. Nothing Flagon couldn't handle.

"You ready, Flagon?" I asked.

"Just give the word."

"DUCK!" I yelled at Lawrence who dove to the ground. I landed on top of him and generated an invisible shield of protection over us. The gang, not too quick on the uptake, started firing at us instead of at Flagon - not that it made a whole lot of difference, because Flagon had transformed. I could tell she'd had her fill for the day, because she did not become a human-sized dragon. In fact, she did not even stop at being an elephant-sized dragon. She took on her full form, which is something you don't want to see if she is mad at you.

The four-gang members behind her, she swept up against a brick wall with her tail. They ended up in rather more pieces then the factory specifications called for. She then leapt forward, crushing the leader under her foot, biting another gang member in half and batting yet another up in the air with her wing. The last one started running, screaming, he ended up well done. She took all the parts and carefully placed them in the dumpster and closed it, then returned to human form.

Lawrence had been on the ground with his eyes closed through all of this, and I let him up. He dusted himself off and asked "Where did they go?" Flagon opened the dumpster and he peered in. "I imagine I don't want to know how that happened," he said.

"No, you don't," I replied. We then made our way without further incident.

Our destination turned out to be a boarded-up building. Lawrence looked fearfully all around before he led us around back, where a window had been jimmied open. We all clambered through. The inside was a bit of a labyrinth also. Eventually, we ended up at a closed door, on which Lawrence knocked. We heard a muffled "come in."

Inside was a very disheveled Arthur Pessinus sitting at a makeshift table. A number of converted gold items were sitting in front of him.

"You are finding out those have less worth than you thought, aren't you?" I said.

"Yes," replied Arthur. "To the point, they absolutely don't do anybody any good, aside from being a jealously-guarded item that gets you robbed or killed."

"So you came across the Midas paradox really quickly, then. That is good; some people take most of a lifetime to figure it out, because I suppose, they have the wrong motives in mind when they start."

"You mean others have discovered how to turn base metal into gold before I did?"

"Of course. King Midas' case of it was the first one recorded."

"I thought that was a myth."

"Think again. It was discovered twice in the dark ages; of course they were really hard at work trying to find it, then. One practitioner was hung as a warlock. The other was tortured as a heretic. It didn't do them any good, either. In the machine age it was discovered five more times that I know of. One other was a physicist like you. The rest were inventors in their fields."

"What did the other physicist do?"

"He contaminated the gold with radio activity and claimed he merely discovered a way to extract gold using a nuclear process. The stuff was useless for 100,000 years, so they left him alone."

"So discovering the process is always a curse, then?"

"No. It is only a curse in two cases: greed and humanitarianism."

"That is a strange set of two cases. Any particular linkage?"

"Yes, they are both at the ends of the spectrum for human compassion. A greedy person uses it for massive personal gain and, sooner or later someone does him in to try to gain the secret. That is pretty much a given end point."

"And the other?"

"That is the not-so-obvious one. You are aware the items on your table are useless; can you tell me why?"

92

"They don't improve any body's life, they can't be sold because you can't show where you got them from, and you can't just keep them, because then someone comes after you for them."

"Someone who knows a less than savory use for them, and therefore are not worried about obtaining their full value. So let's say we take care of that problem; we give the poor here an outlet where they can actually sell their gold items. Are their lives improved or not?"

"Most of them would simply indulge in their vices and end up either back here or dead from self-abuse," Arthur said.

"Right, because you are talking dysfunctional members of society to start with. So, let's go one step further to the working poor. Why wouldn't it help them?"

Arthur scratched his head. "You are losing me on that one. Why wouldn't it?"

"Simply because it would not make most of them more industrious. It is 'found' money, and they would have no idea how to put it to good use. You would need a program to not only supply them with funds but to make sure they did something useful to earn those funds, and that leaves out the last problem."

"Which is?"

"Gold is expensive because it is scarce. You make it less scarce, it loses value. You make it a common item, it is worth no more than its industrial applications. Even if every thing else works, you can not improve the Poor's lot in life on this planet by producing a mountain of gold."

Arthur thought about that for a while. "You mentioned some cases where it isn't a curse."

"Anywhere near the middle. The key being you can't get greedy, and you can't save everybody, but used properly, it can either get you were you want to be, and you already have enough in that regard, or allow you to build a foundation that really does some good. That, of course, will require a lot of hands-on management on your part because somebody always gets greedy when there is money to be had."

"Like my sister-in-law?"

"That is one case, yes. If you gave her your house and all of your money, she would still end up a broken and bitter woman and have no idea what she did to deserve that. Your brother really does care for you; she could care less. She was probably hoping you would disappear permanently."

"You are probably right. There are some obstacles to returning

93

home, though. There is at least one gang out there that looks at me like a certain goose."

"They went dumpster diving," Lawrence said.

"Pardon?" Arthur asked.

"They threatened to kill us and stuff our bodies in a dumpster if we did not lead them to you. Something very large and green suddenly appeared and took them apart, then placed the pieces in the dumpster."

"You wouldn't happen to be Dio and Flagon?" Arthur chuckled.

"You have heard of us?"

"The gangs prey on the poor down here, sometimes killing them for entertainment. Understandably, the locals always cheer for somebody who takes one out and, by popular folklore, you have done in a couple."

"In this case, the folklore is correct."

"Well, let's get going home then." Arthur pulled a wallet out of the wall where he had it hidden. "Oh, would you like this stuff?" He said, indicating the various gold items on the table.

"Sure, that would cover our fees quite nicely. Would you like some change from what we get for them?"

"No, I always know where to find more," Arthur, said half-smiling. "So let's hail a taxi."

"In this neck of the woods? Dream on," I replied.

Lawrence looked uncertain of what he should do.

"None of that Lawrence, you are coming with us. I am going to make good use of your services," Arthur said.

We walked down the alleyway, past the deluxe hotel accommodations and on to the fine bistro where we had spent the last couple of days. As luck would have it, there was a squad car out front. I assumed I knew the reason. Two police emerged with Sarah.

"Well if you see him ma'am, please contact us."

"That I will, officer"

"For whom are they looking?" I asked.

"Arthur Pessinus," Sarah said without batting an eye.

"Gentlemen, you are in luck. I am about to save you days of investigative effort," I said.

"Don't tell me, you are Arthur Pessinus, right?" One of the policemen asked sarcastically.

"No, I am Dio, Private Detective," I said, showing them my badge. "I have business cards, too, but they don't hold up well around here."

"I'll bet," said the officer. "So you know where Arthur Pessinus is located?"

"Yes, two feet in front of you. Arthur, would you mind showing them your ID?"

Arthur did so, and one of the cops checked it out. "Well, Mr. Pessinus, may we offer you a ride home?"

"Only if my friends can come along. Otherwise I will wait for the next bus."

Well the police did not look happy about that, but they wanted to get this over with. The back seat only fits three, so I volunteered to have Flagon sit on my lap. She gave me a look like I'd better not enjoy it. I already knew better than that. Since the back seat was getting 'wiffy' in a hurry, we drove on with the windows down.

"So what happened?" One of the policemen asked Arthur.

"I came to a place in my work where I needed time to think, and, since it would effect the poor, I wanted to understand what their condition is. Somehow, a gang got wind of who I was. I believe it was the 'Screeches', and they were looking to kidnap me for ransom. I had to hide out. Dio and his assistant freed me."

"And the gang?" The policeman asked.

"They are not a factor anymore," I replied.

"Do I want to know what that means?"

"How much do you like paperwork?" I asked.

The policeman was saved the embarrassment of asking anything further, as we had reached our destination. Much to the policemen's relief, we piled out of their car. I figured it was going to get a thorough disinfecting at end of shift today.

We went up to Arthur's door, he felt no need to knock. In retrospect probably not the best of thoughts, they could have used some warning. Anyway, four odorous and very dirty people entered his formerly spotless hallway. A maid screamed, and the butler came up to bar our way.

"See here, I don't know how you got in, but you must leave immediately, or I will be forced to summon the constables!"

"No need, Jives, don't you recognize me?" Arthur said.

"Master Pessinus? What happened?"

"Long story, Jives, and I will be in a better mood to tell it after a shower and a change of clothes. My friends also."

"Yes, sir. Immediately sir." Jives ran off to set things up.

Mrs. Pessinus started up from across the room. "Arthur," she gushed, "we were so worried about you. We were searching for you from the day you disappeared. Not a stone was left unturned. We even hired a private detective to try and find you!"

"Stuff it, Linda," Arthur said. "How is Alice?"

"She will be anxious to see you. Did you want a chance to clean up first?" His brother asked.

"Yes, please," Arthur, said.

Jives returned with staff, changes of clothes and towels. Before we were led off I couldn't resist, I waved at Linda and said, "Hey toots, how's it going?" The look on her face was well worth the price of admission.

A half hour later, cleaned and dressed in clean clothes, we all emerged and went back to the living room. Jives had libations ready. Alice was there, and she immediately ran up to and hugged her uncle. "I missed you too, sweetheart. More than anything else I left behind."

Linda turned several shades of red when she saw who I was. She probably figured I was the reason Arthur could see through her theatrics. She thought wrongly, not that it changed anything. She caught me alone for a minute. (Man does that woman have an ugly mug when she gets mad.)

"You worked for two days. Here is $1,000 to cover it. You are fired. Get out. Take your sleazy secretary with you."

"I am working for Arthur these days; you will have to take it up with him."

"I hired you, I make that decision."

"Alice hired me, and if you don't have the guts to tell Arthur, I certainly will, on my way out the door."

"Go ahead. I will deny everything."

I pulled out my pocket tape recorder and played the conversation back for her. There is wonderful clarity on the newer models, although Linda did not appear to be enthusiastic over the improved tone qualities.

"What is this, blackmail?"

"No, I have no intention of making any use of it except to back up my account, should you press the issue."

"So how much do you want?"

"You weren't listening. I have already been paid. Mr. Pessinus will let me know when he does not need me any more. Oh, and I would be very, very careful about insulting Flagon. She does not take that lightly."

I made my way back to the living room. "Well, Arthur, will there be anything else?"

"No, I imagine you have things to catch up on. And I can always get in contact with you if I need you," Arthur said.

96

"That you can. Good luck with your foundation. If you need any recommendations for people to work with, I know a couple of very good ones."

Alice came up and gave me a hug. "Can I come see you?"

"Sure honey, but bring an adult with you this time or just give us a call, and we will come over, okay?"

We took our leave, and a taxi and headed over to Seymour's place. Since we were previous customers, he was happy to see us.

"So, are we buying or selling today?" Seymour asked.

"I have a couple of really nice items for you," I said, and pulled out the gold.

"This is amazing stuff. Quite an artist, whoever created these. Best I can give you is their gold value in cash, though. I can give you some extra should I be able to sell these on the art market. Much as I hate to say it, I need proof of ownership, though."

I gave him the invoice from the Arthur Pessinus job.

"This will do. Let me weigh it, I will be right back."

He came back out. "It comes to $65,000 dollars. Must have been one heck of a job you did for him."

"It was."

He made a copy of the invoice, had me sign some paperwork and handed me a check for $65,000. We took it to Flagon's bank since she was the only one with any money, and she took out enough to cover everything I owed plus $1,000 cash. Somehow I figured I was buying her dinner again.

Jasper, of course, was happy to see his pay. He started telling us that it was a good thing we coughed up the dough since he had a taker for the office space at double the rent. That would have had more clout if our whole floor were not vacant.

We let ourselves into the office; it felt good to be home.

"So where did you want me to take you tonight? I asked.

"Whatever gave you that idea?" Flagon asked.

"The extra $1000 beans you pulled out."

"Well, now that you mention it, I am hungry."

"Good, there is this great new-age salad bar I have been waiting to try."

Flagon just looked at me blankly.

"Just kidding. How about that new one: 'Full Side O' Beef'?"

"Is that the one with the three-pound steak.'

"Yeah, and if you can eat it all, it is free."

"Well I am going to be a cheap date tonight then."
I grabbed my hat, and we headed out the door.

19
62